THE COST OF GOOD INTENTIONS

This is a work of fiction. Names, characters, places and incidents are the product of the author's imagination or are used fictitiously. Any resemblance to actual persons, living or dead, events, or locales is entirely coincidental.

Copyright © 2023 By Samuel B Lambe

All rights reserved. No part of this book may be reproduced or used in any manner without written consent of the copyright owner except for the use of quotations in a book review.

First paperback edition June 2023

Cover design by nskvsky

ISBN 9798398471373

Published by Amazon KDP

The time is always right to do what is right-

Martin Luther King Jr

CHAPTER 1

COLE

I remember one of my last days in Nod. My bloodshot hazel eyes strained open to the sight of creased sheets. My head was aching as I gingerly got up to silence the monstrosity that was my alarm clock. I had gotten into the habit of moving the clock out of reach as I used to have real problems getting up in the morning.

After years of diagnosing myself as anything but a 'morning person' I stumbled upon an article that gave tips on becoming one.

There were 8 instructions:

1. Get a sleep schedule.
2. Improve your bedtime routine.
3. Move your alarm to avoid hitting snooze.
4. Eat better.
5. Get regular exercise.
6. Enjoy the daylight.
7. Get a sleep study.
8. Treat a sleep disorder.

Out of those 8 I followed rule 3, religiously.

It was 5:01 when I smashed the pressure pad to silence the old, red clock. The wooden drawers beneath shuddered from the force. I slipped into my soft grey slippers and began to drag my feet to the bathroom. I turned on the faucet and heard the cry of water traveling through the old pipes, before the eventual splutter found itself in my rusty sink. I splashed icy water onto my face.

Growing up I was optimistic, seeing the world through a lens that always seemed to be focused on the possibility of all that could be rather than the reality of the present situation. In all that possibility there was never one time when I considered that I would be buttoning up a collared shirt in a room where even the paint wanted to leave.

I buttoned up my grey blazer and picked up my old leather satchel.

I had six flights of stairs to descend before reaching the sidewalk, where my blue bike was chained to the metal railing. It was still dark, and all the roads were deserted as I struggled along my morning commute to my personal hell. It was a 15-minute ride before I eventually caught a glimpse of the polished glass building. I chained my bike up and entered.

The inside of the building was immaculate. You could see your reflection in each floor tile, the glass exterior meant that you could see the cobble stone courtyard on the back side of the building.

Each blade of grass seemed to be hand cut to an exact millimetre measurement.

Upon entering the building, the first thing you notice is the marble coated desk with the word "reception" proudly displayed in silver steel lettering.

Behind the desk was Isa, the receptionist. She was a middle-aged blonde woman. A broad smile was plastered to her face as she looked up to greet me.

"Good morning, Cole"

The Cost of Good Intentions

"Morning Isa," I replied, matching her smile whilst waiting for her to give me my access card.

"You get up to anything fun last night?"

"Oh, you know, the usual. Got home to my mansion, parked the Porche in garage 5, had my butler feed me grapes while I bathed. Then at around 23:00 I thought how excited I am to come to work in the morning. Nothing too fancy."

She giggled and handed me my pass.

"You have a good day, and try to do something more entertaining tonight, okay?"

"Will do," I smiled.

I swiped my card and made my way through the metal turnstiles, towards the elevator.

I pressed the up arrow on the keypad beside the stainless-steel doors and waited patiently until the doors opened with a rhythmic ding-dong. I pressed the button that would take me up to floor 23, the penthouse.

The doors closed and I began my ascent, but I couldn't have felt worse.

When those doors opened, I would have to face 10 hours of the last thing I wanted to be doing.

I didn't plan for it to end up like that, obviously, but that's just the way life goes sometimes.

That's what everyone told me, "Cheer up Cole, life could be worse, you could be homeless- or worse, dead."

I remember hearing those exact words from at least 5 people in the 5 months before.

I took a deep breath as the elevator slowed to a halt and the doors opened.

The Cost of Good Intentions

I walked to my desk. You could tell this is where the company saved its money. Each singular desk was sectioned into 4 smaller ones. The office was empty, but when it did fill up, we would be sitting on top of each other, like sardines in a tin.

My desk was strategically placed right next to my boss's office. When I started working there, I was told that that was the desk that all the new employees started at. That way if I had any questions, I didn't have to walk a lot to get there.

There had been at least 50 new employees hired since then, and I'd never moved.

"Cole? COLE?"

I glanced up to find that Elon was standing right in front of me.

"I've been talking to you for the last 10 minutes, but clearly whatever is in that book of yours is more important than the fact that I'm having a mid-life crisis."

I couldn't help but smirk. Elon was only 27. "Sorry, I was just reading about the cure to premature mid-life crises. It did seem rather important."

"Listen Cole, sarcasm is the lowest form of whit; everyone knows that," he said while trying to be serious, but I could tell he wanted to laugh. Elon and I had been best friends for 12 years, I knew him like the back of my hand.

"Now that you're done being an asshole, what am I supposed to do about the Beck situation?"

"What Beck situation?"

"The one I've been telling you about for the last 10 minutes!"

The Cost of Good Intentions

He let out a deep sigh and for the first time he broke eye contact to look directly behind me. I didn't even have to turn to know that Malcolm was coming. It wasn't often that I felt relief, especially when being interrupted by Malcolm, but I did.

"As usual I catch the two of you doing anything but work, why am I not surprised?" He asked with the sternest expression that a 5'8 obese man could give. The relief left.

"Mole, I need you in my office, now," he snorted at this, like this was the funniest thing that anyone had ever said. I didn't react, I was used to it.

"No problem, Malcolm," I rolled my eyes to Elon as I got up.

For all the time I'd been there I never saw Elon back down from Malcolm, and that time wasn't any different.

"His name is Cole, asshole. How would you like it if everyone just ran around calling you names all the time, when all you could do was just stand there and take it?"

"Cole, my office."

I gave Elon a thankful look. He understood what that meant to me. Malcolm didn't like when anyone stood up to him, and Elon didn't like backing down, especially since he always seemed to get away with it.

I began to slowly force my feet across the hard tiled floor, they squeaked as they were forced forward by whatever will I had left. The sound echoed through the office, almost perfectly expressing the sound hiding itself inside my voice box.

I watched Malcolm walk into his office, he was only a couple of steps ahead of me, but he still let the door swing in my face instead of holding it open while I caught up.

The Cost of Good Intentions

That was his way of showing who was in charge, just in case I had forgotten.

I couldn't help but remember reading about the time that Nelson Mandela hailed the impact of the New Zealand rugby teams Haka. The Haka was a ritual dance done before the teams kicked off, many had just thought it tradition, but Mandela understood its use as an intimidation tactic. He had claimed that New Zealand won a large portion of their games before the game even started, because they were in the other team's mind before a ball had been touched.

I felt like that as I pushed the wooden door open to enter the dark office.

All the brown blinds were closed.

Malcolm was already seated in his oversized chair, behind his oversized desk. The walls behind him were covered with pictures of him, mostly shaking hands with various men. There were a few of him smiling whilst holding trophies, and some where he is playing football.

He looked a lot younger there, the biggest noticeable difference was that in most of the pictures he had a full head of hair.

His desk was bare besides his laptop and a metal cylindrical container holding a dozen black pens.

"Sit down Mole," he gestured to a hard metal chair that was on the other side of his desk.

"I'd rathe-"

"I said sit, Mole."

I walked over and reluctantly took a seat.

"You look like shit."

"Look, if you only called me in here to insult me, I'm just going to get back to work if that's alright."

"That's just the thing Mole, you won't be getting back to work, will you? I've been looking at the numbers from last month and you're down at the bottom. You haven't been following the system, and it shows, the numbers don't lie. You walk in here with bloodshot eyes every morning and stare at a blank screen all day. The calls don't make themselves Mole. Do you think I don't see these things? Do you think I don't see you talking to Elon all the time?"

He looked straight at me the entire time, never faltering, never breaking eye contact, just breaking me down, piece by piece.

"Now I've tolerated this for long enough, if your numbers don't improve this month, I'm going to have to let you go. I am expecting a 20% increase in your sales."

"20? If I increased by 20%, I would be the top seller, Spencer is always the top, Malcolm, and you know it."

"Well then I suppose he won't be top this month if you want a job, will he?"

"But-"

"No buts, Mole. This was never a discussion, it is my expectation, and either you're going to meet that expectation, or you'll have to find work somewhere else. Now leave, I have work to do, and you do too."

I opened my mouth to respond but decided against it. I was never going to make the situation any better, and I knew it, so I stood up and left his office.

The door closed behind me with a bang. The staff office had filled up, I saw Spencer at his desk sitting with perfect posture. He took a sip from a mug that read, 'Mr Right'.

The Cost of Good Intentions

He waved at me as he put his wireless headset on to begin another day of unmatched success.

I didn't even acknowledge him; I wasn't in the mood.

Elon was still at my desk, talking to Beck.

Elon always had a thing for Beck, and everyone knew it. He had asked her out more times than I could count. She had rejected him each time. She had told him that she was taking some time to focus on herself, but we would always see her hanging around with different men.

Watching the two of them was like watching a movie you've seen 1000 times. You know how it ends, you've had time to analyse the details, the only people who don't seem to know it are the ones in the movie.

On several occasions I had thought,

"Surely he knows how this is going to end." But it never seemed to occur to him. That was one thing I knew; you can never understand the chaos of a heart.

Elon had one hand in his denim jeans pocket, the other ran through his black hair that he had combed back. He was going for a kind of John Travolta look. Rebecca clasped her hands together in front of her, making her look more timid than what she was. Her red blouse complimented her red lips and rosy cheeks, which was highlighted by her long flowing black hair.

I approached the desk and they both stopped talking immediately and looked at me.

"What did that human scrotum want?"

"ELOOOOON!!!" Beck slapped his arm playfully, while she giggled.

"Nothing much, he just wanted to remind me who's in charge."

The Cost of Good Intentions

I had contemplated telling them that I'd all but lost my job. I decided against it. It wouldn't make a difference anyway, not when you work for someone who doesn't ever listen.

"Don't let him get to you Cole, it's all he wants."

"I know, anyway, what did you guys do last night?"

"I ordered some sushi and watched Love Island; I can't get enough of that perfect hunk of a ma-"

"Okay, Okay. I don't think anyone within a one-mile radius wanted to hear that," Elon interrupted, "Cole was clearly just trying to be polite; he doesn't actually care what we did last night Beck," he said playfully.

She rolled her eyes at him and laughed.

I watched them do their usual flirtatious back and forth for a couple of minutes before I had seen enough.

"I'm going to have to ask you guys to take whatever is going on here somewhere else, I've got some work to do."

"Alright, buzzkill," Elon said sarcastically "We'll see you at lunch, Captain Serious."

Rebecca had started walking when Elon stretched his arm out in front of him, made whooshing noises and pretended to fly to his desk like Superman. I stifled a laugh when I heard Malcolm scream his name from across the office.

I sat down at my desk, which had a headset underneath a pile of chocolate wrappers. A lone framed picture was in the corner of my desk. It was a picture of me holding up my degree.

I spent so much money on that piece of paper, and I couldn't find a job that would have paid enough to live a decent life.

The Cost of Good Intentions

That was the trap, and I fell for it. The world told me, "Go to school, apply yourself, work hard, get your degree, it'll be worth it."

I believed it, with all my heart, so I did it all. I went to school, I applied myself, I worked hard, I got my degree, it was not worth it. The system had changed, the rules weren't the same. That golden ticket was barely brass in this market.

The worst part was when I took this job for next to nothing, they didn't stop with the game. It wasn't like someone came up to me and said, "Ha-ha, got you, that's the end."

They carried on.

Promise after promise.

"It gets better, later! The benefits are amazing! In just 5 years you can climb the ladder and you'll be telling people what I'm telling you!"

The thing about all of those motivational incentives was that they all came with terms and conditions, and it was never a simple, "If you do this, you'll get that."

The only time things were ever that simple was when the odds were not in your favour.

CHAPTER 2

The clock struck 13:30. I had made it to lunch and the severity of my hangover was fading, fast. That was my favourite part of the day, it was the first point in the day where I felt good and the last point of the day before I felt like I needed a drink.

I made my way over to the staff canteen. There was a vending machine in the corner of a room filled with 4-seater tables.

I sat in the corner table and pulled my lunch box out of my satchel. I had crisps, fizzy juice, a chocolate and an apple.

"You should at least try to make yourself something that your body can actually use," Elon placed his tray opposite my lunch box.

"Yeah, Cole. I can send you some meal plans if you'd like," Spencer sat next to me. Rebecca soon sat next to Elon.

I looked at Spencer's tray. He had a Greek salad with whole grain pita wedges and fruit. Sometimes I was sure he was just trying to annoy me.

"I'm alright, thanks grandad," I replied as I flicked a couple of crisps into my mouth.

"Okay, keep putting that garbage in your body, but don't come calling me when you're needing assistance getting up the stairs."

"Why would I need help getting up the stairs?"

"From the tuberculosis you'll contract from your poor diet!"

Everyone but Spencer burst into laughter.

The Cost of Good Intentions

"I don't think that's how tuberculosis works Spence," I said when I had stopped laughing.

Sometimes It's hard to imagine that someone like Spencer could say things like that, this wasn't the first time. A couple days before he had been arguing with someone for 2 hours straight because he was convinced that in restaurants they wrapped all the pastries in tin foil before putting them in a microwave to add extra crunch.

After putting the theory into the internet, and seeing the results, he still wasn't convinced.

"Of course, they won't show you the truth, the restaurants wouldn't want their secret exposed, otherwise anyone could replicate their product. That is marketing 1-oh-1," he stormed off before the other person could get a word in edge wise.

The first time I heard what Elon and I call a "Spencer," was two years ago.

I needed the toilet, so I got up and while I was walking towards the restroom, I saw that Spencer was looking at flying lessons.

The next day I overheard him talking to someone.

"Really, how hard can it be? You just put the keys in the ignition, start it, and take off."

"A car and a plane are not the same thing Spencer."

"Why not? It's basically a car with wings."

"There are a lot more factors to consider with a plane."

"Like what?"

"Like gravity, for example."

"Gravity? That only affects humans. Insurance companies just tell you it affects everything else to increase their premiums. It's marketing 1-oh-1."

It was when Spencer said that I finally understood that the only thing he was good at was this job. He didn't have anything else going for him, and if it wasn't for his job, he would be screwed.

Me and Spencer became good friends after he took it upon himself to help me improve my pitch to potential clients. It was a win-win, I improved my pitch and he had an opportunity to have the one thing he never had, and always wanted, a friend.

We just started talking at work a bit more, about general things like the weather.

Then one day he actually took a break, instead of working through lunch, and came to sit at the table with me, Elon and Rebecca.

Nobody broke stride, we all just got on like we had been having lunch together for years.

I was thinking about all that while slurping the last bit of the now empty can of juice.

Thinking about the fact that if it wasn't for those people, sitting at that table with me, I would have probably quit that job. Who knows where I would have been?

Elon gave me a look that let me know he wanted to speak to me alone.

I had obliged by packing my lunch box away, standing up, and saying that I was going to get back to work. Even though there was still 15 minutes left for lunch.

Spencer decided to do the same.

"I can't bear to sit here and eat this nutritious lunch for one more second when I know my best friend is to go to war with the beast that is cold calling," Elon said sarcastically before we left, and he walked with me to my desk.

The office was empty when he asked,

"So, what do I do with this Rebecca situation? It's almost time."

"I still have no idea what you're talking about."

"Bro," he looked annoyed, "we are supposed to go out tonight, but I have a date with someone I met online. I don't know what to do!"

"Was this what you were trying to tell me this morning? Wait, how is this a mid-life crisis on any level?"

"Well, cause Beck is like my wife, and it's a common thing for men to have constant thoughts of infidelity during a mid-life crisis."

"I completely understand, there's just one small detail you seem to be forgetting."

"Which is?"

"You and Beck aren't married. You aren't even dating."

"Those are small technicalities, Cole. I don't think anyone can deny that we belong together. You seem to be missing the point though, what do I do?"

"If I were you, I would just tell her. It's Beck, I am sure she will understand. She is always the one rejecting you."

"You could have stopped at the understanding part, no need to break my heart, Cole," he gave me an appreciative smile, patted my back, and left me alone.

The Cost of Good Intentions

I didn't see him for the rest of the day, because I always stayed a bit later than him as I needed the money.

Time seemed to fly, I knew I was supposed to be focusing on getting more clients, but I could only think of how excited I was for Elon. I would never say it to him, but I'd been waiting for the day that he decided to take a chance and meet someone new. I wondered what she was like, how long they'd been talking, when he even registered for online dating.

Don't get me wrong, I liked Beck, but when you watch someone continue to hurt your best friend it gets harder to understand why he kept trying in the first place.

Einstein once said that the definition of insanity is doing the same thing over and over again and expecting different results. I don't think he was talking about dating at that point, but he could have been.

I wanted better for my best friend, even if that meant that he had to leave behind the one thing he believed was his happiness.

I glanced at my watch, it was 17:00, and time for me to leave. I removed my headset with shaking hands, put it on the desk, grabbed my satchel and made my way to the exit.

When I reached the reception desk, I handed my key card to Isa and wished her a good evening.

I unchained my bike and began to ride to the corner store, to get some drinks for the night.

When I got to the store, I opened the door and began to weave my way through the small store's aisles. I picked up a bottle of vodka from the 3rd and final aisle, and walked to the checkout, getting crisps from just beside the counter.

The Cost of Good Intentions

I put everything on the counter and began to search for my wallet in my satchel.

The cashier didn't acknowledge me, he seemed preoccupied by something underneath the counter. I leaned forward to see he had a small television there and he was watching the news.

"Anything important?" I asked, more to get his attention than anything.

"Sorry, sir. They were just saying there is some heavy rain due later today and everyone should stay inside tonight."

He scanned the vodka and crisps, I paid and left. While I unchained my bike I looked up, there wasn't a cloud in the sky. I shrugged off the thought and started cycling home.

When I got to my apartment I went to the "kitchen", which was just a stove and some cupboards in the same space as my bedroom.

I got a glass and opened the bottle of vodka before I poured myself a glass.

A spring stabbed into my lower back as I tried to lay on my bed. I readjusted myself, flicked on the television and took a sip of my drink. Instant relief. My hands stopped shaking; my stomach thanked me. My head rewarded me with a rare positive thought.

I started watching, "The Fresh Prince of Bel Air", sipping away in pleasure. Life was good at this moment, right here.

I was 20 minutes into watching the episode where Will is challenged by a college football player to a drinking contest, when I needed another drink. I returned and put the bottle next to the bed.

3 drinks later I needed the toilet. I got up and stumbled to the bathroom, unzipped my trousers and began to urinate.

The Cost of Good Intentions

About 15% found its way to the bowl. The other 85% was either on the seat or on the floor. I broke off some toilet paper and tried to clean the mess. I was struggling so I did what I could before flushing the urine-soaked toilet paper down the toilet.

I turned on the faucet, washed my hands, then grabbed a towel and began to dry them while I looked at myself in the mirror. My bald head had a sharp glean to it when reflecting the bathroom light. My eyes creased at the side when I started to laugh.

I wasn't too sure why I was laughing, it just felt right in that moment. My moment was cut short by the sound of the latch stopping someone from opening my door. I wasn't expecting anyone.

"COLE!!!"

I knew that voice.

I walked to the door and unlatched it to see Beck, in a long black coat, staring at me. To say I was confused would be an understatement. I had so many questions which she answered, in one simple sentence, before I even got to ask them.

"We are going to spy on Elon's date."

I threw on a thick black jacket, grabbed my wallet, keys, and phone and we were on our way.

I had to hold on to the railing tightly to stop myself from falling while we made our way down the concrete stairs. I didn't think Beck noticed, until we got to the bottom, and she turned to me.

"You look like shit."

"Can everyone stop telling me that?" I slurred.

The Cost of Good Intentions

"Who's everyone?"

"Never mind, let's just get going, and maybe you can tell me why exactly you want to spy on Elon instead of pretending that I am the one acting weirdly."

She wasn't too sure how to respond.

The 3 of us had a pact that we had made almost 4 years ago. We had said that if ever we needed each other's help, we just had to ask, and it would be done. No exceptions.

That was one of those moments. I just wasn't too sure why she needed my help? Why couldn't she just go alone?

Beck turned and began walking without saying another word.

We walked 5 blocks before we turned onto the street where Elon stayed.

He lived in a quiet cul-de-sac; all the houses were well sized with beautiful green gardens. Flower beds lined white picket fences. Well maintained streets gently curved onto neat sidewalks which housed red mailboxes. The streetlights illuminated empty streets. Every house had a built-on garage, one was opening as a Range Rover was waiting to pull in.

Elon had inherited his house from his grandfather. His grandfather never got along with Elon's dad, Dave.

Dave got Elon's mom, Yvonne, pregnant when they were both 18. Dave couldn't deal with the responsibility, so when Yvonne told him that she was expecting he immediately pushed for her to get an abortion. She refused, so Dave did what most scared 18-year-old boys did. He went home after that conversation, packed a bag, and ran. Nobody could find him; he didn't even leave a note. All he left behind was a pregnant girl carrying his child.

Elon's grandparents helped Yvonne raise Elon, because Yvonne came from a poor family.

When Elon was 12, he started asking questions. He didn't understand why his "dad" was so much older than all the other dads, so they told him. After he knew the truth, Elon started looking for his real dad, but it was hard to find someone who had no real ties to anything. One day when Elon was 14, he was watching the news and he saw a picture of a man who was wanted for multiple thefts. Yvonne turned the television off and rushed to speak to Elon's grandparents.

Two days later, there was a knock on the door, Elon's grandfather answered, and the man from the news stood outside. Yvonne quickly grabbed Elon, who heard a lot of shouting before he was shoved into his room and the door was locked.

20 minutes later there were red and blue lights flashing through the window, accompanied by the sound of loud sirens. His door was kicked down before a team of heavily armoured police officers swarmed into the room. They checked every corner of the room, swinging the cupboards open in the process, before one shouted, "CLEAR!"

The word was repeated 4 times, from different parts of the house, before a police officer escorted Elon out of the room, and they headed towards the front door. He looked left into the kitchen before the officer managed to stop him.

A scream escaped as he saw his mother's lifeless body in a pool of blood, a cell phone was held firmly in her hand.

The Cost of Good Intentions

Dave had killed Yvonne and Elon's grandmother. The doctor's managed to save his grandfather, who moved them out of that house and into the cul-de-sac. He wrote a will, leaving everything he owned to Elon.

The police had found Dave the day after he had murdered Yvonne and Elon's grandmother, his body floating in a nearby lake. Elon's grandfather lived 5 years after that, before he got severely ill, was admitted to hospital and died of a heart attack. Elon has stayed in the same house ever since.

When we got to Elon's house, which was at the end of the cul-de-sac, the lights were all off.

"He's not here, Beck."

"I know that Cole, I just need you to see that he isn't going to come home while I get inside."

"What? Are you mad? Why would I ever consider doing that?"

"No exceptions, remember?"

"This is a stretch, Beck, and you know it."

"Come on Cole, I know it's a lot. I just have to."

"Have to what?"

"I have to just leave something of mine, so his date finds it if he tries to bring her home."

"Beck I-"

I couldn't finish my sentence because Beck spotted headlights coming towards us. She grabbed my wrist and pulled me behind the nearest bush. I practically fell, considering it was taking all my concentration to stand up straight.

The Cost of Good Intentions

I was about to express my annoyance when she put her hand over my mouth and gestured for me to keep quiet before she slowly removed her hand. I kept quiet when she did.

Elon's Aston Martin pulled up. He parked it outside the garage, which no doubt held his Hummer.

We watched silently as he got out the car and walked to the other side of the car to open the door. A petite blonde stepped out. She was wearing a black dress to flaunt her curves.

"I can't cook as well as the restaurant, but I'm sure my drinks are better, Zoe," Elon said as he extended his hand for her to take.

"I would hope so, I don't like being let down, Elon," Zoe said as she took his hand, and they walked to the house.

I looked to Beck. She looked furious, and before I could do a thing she was storming toward the house.

I really didn't understand any of it. I didn't know why she was so upset.

I didn't follow. I just waited; I didn't have to wait long before Beck came out with tears streaking her face. Zoe followed closely with Elon just behind her, trying to get hold of her hand, and failing. Elon saw me.

"Cole? What are you doing here?"

Beck was walking away from us, and fast, I wasn't sure what to do.

"I'll explain later," I said before I used all my concentration to jog towards Beck.

I was calling for her while jogging, she didn't even turn, didn't slow her pace. I caught up to her just at the beginning of the street. I grabbed her wrist and turned her to face me. She just broke into a hysterical cry.

"He's such an asshole, Cole."

"I don't understand, what happened?"

"You saw what happened, he brought that girl home Cole. He knows how I feel about him."

"Beck, I know you're a bit upset, and maybe it isn't what you want to hear, but you can't keep playing with people's feelings and expect them to wait until you're ready for something more serious."

She stopped crying. Her face was filled with a mixture of anger and confusion.

"Is that what you think? Is that what he told you? Cole, I have been up front with Elon from the start. I have wanted to be with him for years, but every time I ask him to be my boyfriend, HE tells ME that he isn't ready for something serious."

"Wait, what? But what about all the guys you're always with?"

"Not my smartest idea, but I just went out with those guys, told them my story and hung around them to make Elon jealous."

"How come I never knew this?"

"You never speak to me, aside from the times when we are all together."

My drunken mind swam through all the memories it had the ability to summon and concluded that she was telling the truth. I never really asked her side of the story.

I remembered a time when Elon had randomly come to visit me. He told me that he just wanted to drink and forget the night. He told me that Beck had rejected him again, and I never questioned it, not once. I got a bottle of vodka, and we drank the night away. I normally don't remember a lot from those types of evenings, but I can never forget what I told him that night.

I laughed as I said, "Bro, the day she says yes, I am pretty sure the world will end."

He laughed because he was drunk. The next morning, I could tell he didn't remember what I had said, and I always felt guilty about it.

I didn't know it then, but now I find that statement ironic. You see, it wasn't when she said yes that the world ended. It was when I found out that after all that time, she had been saying yes, the entire time, that life as we knew it did.

CHAPTER 3

I couldn't believe what I had heard, didn't know how to respond, I stared blankly at Beck for what seemed like an eternity. My mind was malfunctioning, not sure what was real and what wasn't.

Stuck on one single word. Why?

Why would he lie to me about this? It didn't make any sense. I had known Elon since we were 15.

Maybe we didn't grow up together, but it sure felt like we did. I couldn't wrap my head around it all, and I wouldn't have the time to.

A 12-car convoy sped across a street a couple corners away. They must have been travelling in excess of 120mph. It caught mine and Beck's attention.

Two moments later we watched another 6-car convoy follow, and another one a minute later.

A light rain began to start, quickly becoming heavier. It wasn't long before we were caught in a downpour. We both began to run, straight to Elon's house.

We tried the door handle, it was unlocked. We rushed inside, slamming the door behind us.

I was breathing heavily, so was Beck. Both of us were soaking wet.

Elon appeared from his living room, looking a bit confused.

"What happened to you two?"

"It's absolutely pouring outside, can't you see?" Beck practically barked at him.

The Cost of Good Intentions

Considering the rain outside it was dead silent in his house. The loudest sound was the television in the living room.

"We're going to have to stay here, until it calms down," I couldn't bring myself to look at him, not after what I had found out. I don't think he noticed.

"No problem, I'll go get you guys some towels and fresh clothes," he didn't wait for any response, he just turned and walked up the stairs. He returned a couple of minutes later and handed me a towel and a shirt that read, 'this guy has two thumbs,' with a picture of a monkey smiling and pointing at itself.

He handed Beck one that said, 'Super Hot,' with a picture of a chilli.

She wasn't amused, instead she just walked to one of Elon's three bathrooms and shut the door.

I changed into the shirt, handing him my old clothes in the process.

He just smiled at me before leaving to put the clothes in the dryer.

I went into his lounge. It was bigger than my entire flat. There was a huge wooden table in the middle of the room. Intricate carvings covered the surface. It was on top of a carpet made of tiger skin.

There was a six-seater black leather corner couch which faced his wall-mounted 82" television.

There was a leather chair facing the wood stacked fireplace. The house was exceptionally clean for something of its size, but then again, Elon had a cleaner 5 days a week.

The Cost of Good Intentions

The news was on, I sat on the couch, I made sure I was fully dry before doing so. Elon and Beck walked in, neither of them looked happy.

He handed me a blanket and asked if I wanted a drink.

"Just a beer, if you have." I needed one after all that had happened that night. I was sure the drama with the two of them wasn't finished and I wasn't going to go through it sober.

Elon left and came back with a six pack of beer.

I cracked open a can and gulped down half of it before I overly focused on the news, so I didn't accidently get dragged into a conversation that I wasn't ready to have.

The news reporter was a man in his 40s. He had dark brown hair, and a bad stutter. His name was Carl.

He was talking about global warming. It was all that was on the news those days. The temperatures fluctuated constantly; extreme weather was the norm. If it wasn't a record high, it was a record low. The winter before we had had snow for two weeks, followed by a spell of the hottest weather recorded in the past 70 years.

A clip with the headline, "climate crisis turns chaotic." played on the television. It showed a protest of the latest plans to discontinue petrol car sales. There were at least 10000 people in the video. A camera flew above head, slowly making its way from the front of the crowd to the back. There were armoured police officers with riot gear at the front of the protest. Holding back the furthest forward protestors who were trying to break their way through to fight with protestors who supported the plans.

The people against the plans held up signs. One read, "Climate change = Natural cycle,"

Another said, "The world will recover, my pocket won't."

It wasn't long before everything on the screen turned to chaos. It started when one person managed to break through the police line. The woman was tackled to the ground by a broad-shouldered officer. There was a loud gasp before stones started flying in the officers' direction.

Hundreds of people started rushing forward, before a thick cloud of smoke was seen at the far-right corner of the screen. The officers were slowly moving forward, pushing the crowd back.

Some people began to flee, others carried on throwing rocks.

The angle changed to show a burning car with people running, some were holding their face.

A loud bang was heard, and screams echoed through the speakers before the clip was cut.

"We apologise for any distress that clip might have caused," Carl said while he flicked through some papers on his desk, without looking at the camera.

"And now, time for the weather, over to you Penny."

A short, freckled woman came onto the screen pointing to various points on a map of Nod.

The entire country had giant black clouds covering it. Little lightning bolts were accompanied by rain droplets underneath the clouds.

"As you can see, the weather is being dominated by an extreme low-pressure system, which has just begun to bring a series of widespread storms across the country. The weather will last a couple of days before we are treated to a spell of warmth as a high-pressure system moves in from the west."

The Cost of Good Intentions

A list came up with the various temperatures, everywhere was just around 1°C.

I cracked open another beer as the television suddenly turned off. I looked left to see Elon holding the remote.

"Look, we can sit here all night and not say another word to each other, but I think we can agree that it isn't going to help. We're going to need to talk about what happened here tonight."

"Let's just leave it until the morning," I said before I took another sip.

"No, Cole, let's not wait for tomorrow, let's start right now. Firstly, I'd like to just say that you look like shit."

"Okay, that's definitely been established today," I scoffed.

"Secondly, what were you guys doing at my house?"

"We were just passing by and decided to drop in to see how your date was going."

"Both you and I know, that's not the truth Cole."

"The truth? You're really going to lecture me about the truth?"

"What's that supposed to mean?" he raised his voice with that question.

"Don't worry about it, I don't want to put you through the pressure of having to come up with more lies."

"What lies? Cole, what are you talking about?"

"I can't actually believe you," Beck broke her silence, "I had to tell Cole the truth tonight. You painted me as a villain for years, Elon. I can't believe I actually liked you."

The colour drained from Elon's face. He knew I knew. He was embarrassed.

"Cole…I…"

The Cost of Good Intentions

"Why'd you lie, Elon? All those nights you came to me looking like a broken man, you really made me believe that you were the victim in all this. The foolish victim, so drawn by the hope of a pure love that you couldn't see the reality that stared you right in the face."

"I was embarrassed, okay? I was ashamed of myself. I thought that if you knew the truth, if you knew that I was turning down someone who I did like, but couldn't bring myself to date, you wouldn't like me anymore. I told myself that it would just be the one little lie, but it grew into so much more. I came to you after the first night that I went on a date with someone after turning down Beck. I couldn't deal with the guilt, I know we weren't dating, but I felt like I was cheating on someone I knew would probably be there when I was finished messing around. It carried on though, girl after girl, and after a while my guilt changed. I no longer felt guilty about the "cheating", I felt guilty that I liked it. I had a system, a routine, and I was okay for the first time in a while. I didn't want to mess everything up."

"The part that hurts me the most is that you lied to me. I've always told you the truth, Elon, no matter how hard it was for me."

"I know, and I'm sorry, Cole. Really, I am."

I looked at Beck who was looking at Elon. Her eyes glistening while she fought to hold back tears.

"So that's all I am to you? A back-up for when you decide you need someone to love you when you're done with everybody else."

She looked like she was about to leave, Elon grabbed her wrist before she could.

The Cost of Good Intentions

"I never meant for it to come out like this."

"Well, Elon, you don't get that luxury with lies. Lies don't play by the rules that you set, they don't disappear either. Once you create them, they're always there, hiding in the corner of every room, waiting for the best moments to weave their way out of your grasp."

"I can't say anything but sorry, if anything, I just want you to know that I never meant to hurt you like this. I just want us all to be friends, I can't lose you because I was a coward. Please, just…please."

"It'll take time to heal, it's not going to be the same."

Elon couldn't meet anyone's eyes as the room fell silent.

"It's getting late, you should stay for the night," he said to us both.

I wasn't going to argue, even if it had stopped raining. I wasn't going to try to walk now, it was getting late, and I didn't have my bike.

"Okay," we both agreed.

I took the last sip of my beer before Elon took the empty can from me.

He threw it in the kitchen bin while he led us up the stairs to the guest bedrooms.

He told Beck that the first room on the left would be hers for the night. She didn't say anything before walking in and closing the door. There was a click as the lock latched into place. We walked a bit farther down the passage until we reached a room on the right-hand side of the passage.

"And here's your room bro, give me a shout if you need anything."

I nodded before stepping into the room.

The Cost of Good Intentions

"Cole?"

"What's it?"

"Don't think less of me."

I looked down before I met his eyes, "I don't, bro."

He gave me a wry smile as he closed the door. I turned to the room. There was a 65" Samsung TV on a pure white wall unit. The linen of the queen-sized bed was pressed, so there wasn't a crease in sight. There were two bedside tables, one either side of the bed, each with reading lamps. The right-hand wall had an opening that led to a white tiled bathroom with a giant bath in one corner. A shower was in the opposite corner. Next to the shower was a pure white basin with a framed mirror right on top. There was another opening in the wall that led to a toilet fit for royalty. I never thought that could even be a thing.

The left wall had glass sliding doors that led out to a well sized balcony, that overlooked the flower-dominated 800 square foot garden. The boundaries of the garden were illuminated by multiple lights, shining bright enough to highlight the entirety of the towering trees.

I climbed into the bed and rested my head on the pillow as I looked out, into the garden.

I couldn't help but think how strange the contrast was. 5 blocks separated me from Elon, but we felt worlds apart. In my neighbourhood, you were statistically more likely to get mugged than you were to have a job. Where here, you were more likely to get eaten by a shark than you were to get mugged.

All that change, separated by less than a mile.

I watched as the rain continued to pour heavily, I looked at it until my eyes felt heavy and I fell asleep.

CHAPTER 4

I woke the next morning with a splitting headache. The rain had stopped. Small puddles had formed on the wet grass outside. I needed water; my mouth felt like I had eaten a bag of sand. I flung the soft sheets off of me and walked to the bathroom. I gulped down cold water like I hadn't had anything to drink for days. It was so refreshing feeling the water slide down my dry throat. I strained to open my eyes a bit wider as I left the room and made my way to the kitchen.

I walked past Beck's room; the door was still shut. Elon was in the kitchen. His see-through kettle had a blue light shining while steam rose from the spout as water boiled.

"Coffee?" Elon asked with his back turned to me.

"Please," I took a seat on one of the eight highchairs that surrounded a granite countertop.

Elon went to the fridge to get milk, and some orange juice for himself.

He placed a glass into a compartment on the exterior of the silver fridge. He pressed a few buttons before ice dispensed into the glass. He poured himself some juice and took a small sip, letting out a sigh of pleasure.

He put two sugars in my coffee, topped it up with milk and placed the steaming hot cup in front of me.

I was barely through the first sip before my phone rang, making me almost spill my coffee in the process.

Malcolm's name was on the screen.

"Mole, where are you? It's 8:30."

I panicked before remembering it's Saturday.

The Cost of Good Intentions

"It's Saturday Malcolm, I'm not in today."

"Wrong, you weren't in today but nobody else showed up, and we need you."

"I'm not going to be able to make it, Malcolm," I said, trying to sound sorry, but failing.

"That's not good enough, Mole. Now either you get here, or you can start looking for a new job before this phone call ends. We have a system to run here."

I needed the job, I really needed the job, and he knew it. I was so conflicted. One part of me was ready to change into my, now dry, clothes and just go but that part didn't win, and I couldn't stop myself.

"Fuck your system, Malcolm. You run it. I am sick of it, sick of all of it. I refuse to just sit here anymore and let you get away with treating me like shit."

"I'm sorry you feel like that, I never meant to make you feel like that," I could hear the delight in his voice, he was loving every second. He had been waiting for that day for years, the day when he could dismiss me without repercussion.

Anger boiled in me, brimming over the edges of everything rational in my body. I had one moment where I was able to get control of myself. I forced myself to calm down. I wouldn't give him the satisfaction of hearing just how much he had got to me. I hung up the phone before either of us could say another word.

Elon was looking at me, his face was unreadable. He just stared blankly, waiting for an explanation.

"Can you take my letter of resignation in when you go to work on Monday?"

"What do you mean? You can't just quit like that, Cole."

The Cost of Good Intentions

"Why not?"

"What about your bills? you can't afford to do something so drastic."

"Elon, I have sat at the same desk for 6 years, looking out the same window every day. Not one day did I look out and feel anything other than absolute hopelessness. My bills? I can't take care of them if I am dead. That's where I'm headed, at this rate, an early grave. I can't do it anymore; I need a change."

"I never knew you felt like that, Cole."

"I feel like that every day. I don't remember the last time I woke up with a fraction of optimism. The system has broken all the good parts in my body, it's like they want me to run after they broke my legs. I had dreams once, Elon. I wanted to be an artist. I sat in my room drawing pictures for hours every day, until we left high school. I was told, there's no money in that industry, you need to be logical. Well, look where logic has got me. I'm 27 and bald, I live in the worst neighbourhood in Nod. I can't afford most things, hell, I can barely afford to feed myself properly. You and Beck have been my only true source of happiness for years."

"I'm glad we could do that for you," Beck walked into the room in her own clothes, "We are always here for you, Cole. You shouldn't ever feel like you're alone. Remember that."

"Let's go to the lounge, you can finish your coffee, I'll get the laptop so we can start looking for a new job for you," Elon was already on the way.

The Cost of Good Intentions

I really did have good friends, and in that moment, I felt a mixture of fear and anxiety, but I couldn't ignore the tiny sliver of something I hadn't felt in a while. Excitement.

I started up the laptop that Elon had brought, and while it was loading, the television turned on with bold red letters reading, "EMERGENCY ANNOUNCEMENT"

A robotic voice kept repeating, "This is an emergency announcement, everyone is to stay indoors, do not try to go outside. Major danger to life has been detected." It wouldn't stop. Elon pressed several buttons on the remote. It would not stop. We were all up and running to the balcony in Elon's room, to see what was happening outside.

Everything looked normal until I realized that it was still dark.

I didn't know what time it was until I looked at my watch. 9:15. I watched as the second hand on my watch slowly ticked. The watch seemed to be working. I pulled my phone out my pocket. 9:15.

They both couldn't be wrong. Elon and Beck looked from each other to me. They looked like they had realized what I had just realized myself.

If it was 9:15, where was the sun?

My head started spinning so I sat down on Elon's bed. Elon and Beck sat next to me.

"How is this possible? How is any of this possible?" Beck asked, more to herself than to any of us.

"I have no idea, but we don't have time to sit here and think about it, we need to prepare ourselves for the worst," I got up and was walking towards the door.

"Where are you going?" Elon asked.

"We need to find out what's going on, at the least we need food for a couple of days."

"Can you not hear the television, Cole?" The message was still going on repeat.

"Do you have any better ideas?"

"Yes, we listen to the message and stay inside."

"He's right, Cole, we should listen to the message," Beck added.

"For how long? Days? Weeks? Months? Who knows how long this is going to last? The sun it GONE. You know? That big yellow thing in the sky, that provides us with heat?"

"Exactly, provides us with heat! What if you go out there and it's too cold and you instantly freeze?"

"Look outside. If it was that cold everything would be frozen."

"Well then maybe it's just late, you know, with all that global warming stuff. Maybe it's just going to come up later from now on."

"Then why is there an emergency announcement on the television?"

"It could be a terrorist attack, and you could be killed if you go outside. Please, Cole, just stay inside for now. We'll go to the kitchen and do an inventory of what we have, in the meantime."

"One day. That's all the time I am waiting."

We went to the kitchen.

There were 7 eggs, 4 bags of crisps, 2 boxes of cereal, a carton of milk and a loaf of bread. There an abundance of alcohol though, Elon was a collector of all kinds of whisky and wine. His basement cellar had hundreds of bottles that he had picked up over the years. Whenever he had come to my place, he brought a bottle for us to share.

"How do you live in a house like this and have so little food?"

"I order a lot of take-aways, okay?"

"We are really going to have to ration. Who's up for skipping a meal today?"

"I don't mind," Beck said.

"If I have to," Elon groaned.

"Okay, good"

"Do you have your neighbours' numbers, Elon?"

"I do, why?"

"Well, we should call them and see if we can help each other somehow."

"They aren't home."

"Where are they?"

"Holiday, Bill went last week, and Meryl left two days ago."

"Shit! Come on, Cole, think. Think," I said to myself, rubbing my temple with the tips of my fingers. I knew what I needed.

I headed to the cellar, came back, and poured myself a glass of whiskey.

"Really?" Beck couldn't hide her disgust.

"I think better when my head isn't screaming at me," I gulped down the contents of the glass and poured another, "That's better. We need to find all the warmest clothing in the house and put it on. We aren't sure when the electricity is going to go out, but if this goes on, it won't be long with nobody able to run the power stations."

"Good thinking, Cole. Have another glass if it makes you come up with ideas like that," Elon joked.

"Everyone, go through the cupboards in the rooms you stayed in last night."

We split up and went to look for warm clothes.

I got to the room and opened the cupboard. It was overflowing with an assortment of coats, jackets, jerseys, jumpers, t-shirts and trousers.

I couldn't believe the amount of clothing in that cupboard. That was his spare bedroom. Why would anyone need so much? I wasn't going to complain. I looked through the clothes and pulled out a red jumper that had, "Higher" written in bold white lettering, I took off my jacket and put the jumper on.

I found a bag in the bottom of the cupboard. I put in a few of everything before zipping the bag up, slinging it over my shoulder and going to find Elon and Beck.

It felt a bit colder than it had a moment ago. I heard my footsteps tapping against the tiles as I walked down the passage, toward the stairs. Silence.

The emergency message had stopped.

I took a deep breath before continuing to walk through the house. I found Elon and Beck in the lounge.

They had bags of their own, which they had sitting in front of them while they sat of the couch.

Beck looked scared; Elon looked like he was trying to put on a brave face.

I sat down next to them both, Elon handed me a drink.

The Cost of Good Intentions

"What now?" he looked straight ahead as he asked the question.

"Now, we enjoy the last day of our lives,"

I put down my drink, grabbed the bottle off the table, and took a deep swig.

"Wake up, Cole," I felt my body being shaken, "COLE!"

A hard slap followed.

"Shit!" I yelled as I sat up and opened my eyes. Beck was standing, looking down at me.

"Sorry, I didn't mean to hit you that hard, we need to go."

"Go? Where?" I was just getting my bearings. An empty bottle of whiskey was next to me, a metal door was in the room that wasn't there before, a keypad was next to it.

"What's going on?"

"I don't know. I woke up a few minutes before you. Elon is gone, Cole. I am so worried."

I got up gingerly, and walked to the keypad. I knew most of Elon's passwords, they were usually some important date to him. I entered his birthday into the keypad and the metal door raised.

"Let's take a look around."

"Okay."

We made our way through the house. Every room was trashed. The mattresses were flipped, televisions smashed, drawers pulled from various shelves, cupboard doors ripped from their hinges.

The most noticeable, and alarming, thing was that everything was gone. Everything that we could have possibly used had been taken. The room I stayed in was the last one that we checked, and by far the worst hit. The door was left slightly open, a trail of blood was leading into the room.

I put my hand in front of Beck, forcing her to stop. I gestured that I would go first, just in case.

I was careful not to make a sound as I slowly approached the room. My heart was pounding as I got closer. I felt the chaotic beat in my fingertips as I reached for the door handle.

3…

2…

1…

I threw the door open and rushed into the room. Scanning each corner of the room, as fast as I could. My mind felt like it was swimming, my brain felt like it was submerged in liquid as my head swung recklessly from side to side. My brain was in shock, trying to process each detail in the room.

I had assessed that the room was empty the moment I entered, but the blood.

It was everywhere. Hand marks on the walls, footprints on the floor, the sliding door was splashed with it. The bed sheets were absolutely soaked with it. I covered my nose as I got a whiff of the rotten smell. I took a step forward; my breathing was heavy and irate. I felt something underneath my right foot, it squished underneath me. I looked down at the bloody corpse beneath my foot and spewed my guts out. I needed to get out of there.

I rushed to the door, covering my nose, my eyes were blood red and watering as I tried to focus on just escaping that nightmare.

The Cost of Good Intentions

I made it to the hall, and slammed the door shut. Beck wasn't far behind, she was standing hunched over with her hands on her knees. She was standing over a pool of her own vomit. I walked towards her; a trail of bloody footprints being left in my wake.

"It isn't his body, so there is still hope that whoever was in here didn't kill him."

"Oh God, oh God. Cole, what are we going to do? I don't know what to do, I don't. Fuck," She was pacing, staring directly at the ground. Tears began to form in her green eyes. She ran her fingers through her hair before she covered her mouth with both palms. I watched as tears were streaming down her cheeks as she fell to her knees and began pounding the ground.

I caught her fist, before she hurt herself, and pulled her up.

"We can't panic, do you understand? We need to try stay calm and think clearly."

She nodded and began to dry her eyes.

"We need help, Cole. We need to find out what's going on."

I got an idea. I pulled my phone out of my pocket. I had 33% battery left. I got slightly annoyed at myself for not charging my phone but decided that my annoyance wouldn't change anything.

I dialled 999.

The line cut. It didn't even ring once.

"999 is out of service."

I was trying so hard to stay calm, to think what the best thing to do was. It was so hard, because no matter what, I could only think one thing.

We were alone, and I had no idea what to do.

The Cost of Good Intentions

In school they teach you all kinds of things that are supposed to help you in life. You are taught skills to enable you to become a productive member of society, so what happens when that society crumbles?

I couldn't think like that, I couldn't let myself become consumed by this hopelessness. I would die if I did. I decided that we needed to get to my apartment. We needed new clothing, the bags were gone, and I couldn't continue to wear those blood-soaked clothes. The fact that people had got into the house, and out meant that it couldn't be uninhabitable outside.

"We need to get back to my apartment. I have a bit of food and drink there, as well as a change of clothing."

"Okay," that was all Beck could manage to say. Her face was as white as a sheet, she looked dejected.

We headed for the door, neither of us looked anywhere other than straight. We didn't want to see anything else.

When we reached the door, we both zipped up our jackets, and tossed our hoods over our heads.

I opened the door and took a step out, Beck followed closely behind. It was cold, but not nearly as cold as I would have imagined. I reached the street; it was illuminated by the streetlights. The world looked strange, I was so used to the general busyness of everything that the pure lack of life was a humbling experience.

Every garage on the street was open, exposing vacant parking spaces. The only house light that shone was Elon's.

"Where has everyone gone?" Beck came to stand next to me.

"I don't know, but we need to keep moving."

The Cost of Good Intentions

Each time there was a dip in the street it was filled entirely by water. We took care to avoid the puddles, as we weren't sure how deep each dip was. When we had left Elon's neighbourhood, we began noticing house lights. Every second or third house had lit windows.

"Should we check to see if anyone is there?" I stopped in front of the first house we came across with its light on.

"I think we should keep moving. We aren't sure how these people could react to us in these kinds of circumstances, Cole."

"I suppose you're right."

"We can always come back once we've got some supplies, and maybe, some weapons."

We walked quickly and it was only 10 minutes before we stood outside my apartment building.

There were some lights shining from the windows of apartments on different floors, too. I was staring at the building, trying to assess which light belonged to which person, before I could even identify one my eyes drifted.

There was a streetlight shining straight onto the metal railing where my bike should have been. All that was there was my chain, left lying on the floor, cut.

I sighed before we started walking up the stairs.

I opened the door and flicked on the light.

I let out a deep breath, that I wasn't aware I had been holding. Beck latched the door locked while I headed for the "kitchen".

Beck was already in my, "room", packing a new bag of clothing and food supplies. I put my phone on charge and went to help her.

The Cost of Good Intentions

We were packing the last few items of clothing when we heard someone trying to get into the room.

The latch caught the door before the person on the other end closed the door and tried to knock.

I looked at Beck. We both knew that we had to open the door, at some point. We walked slowly towards the door. She stopped at a drawer in the kitchen and slowly opened it. I watched as she carefully pulled out a knife. I wasn't sure either one of us had ever thought we would need to contemplate using a knife, but we didn't have the time to assess our options. Whoever was on the other side of that door knew we were here, and I doubt they were going to leave.

Another knock came, this one slightly harder than the last.

Beck hid behind a wall, holding the knife closely to her chest. Her hands trembling.

I decided to risk a look through the keyhole. It didn't help, at all, all I could see was the person's denim jeans pocket.

Another knock.

My hands covered my mouth to stop a scream from escaping.

When I had calmed down, I put my left hand on the latch, slowly sliding it to the right. It came loose with the faintest of clicks, before I put my right hand on the door handle.

I pressed the handle as hard as I could and yanked the door open. I was halfway out the door when I saw Brad standing in front of me.

He had put his hands in front of his face, to try and protect himself, when he saw me lunging towards him.

"COLE!"

I stopped at once, almost losing my footing whilst trying to regain my balance.

"What the fuck, man?" he straightened himself up.

"Come inside, quickly," I moved aside and let Brad into my apartment, when he was inside, I poked my head out and gave the stairwell a quick onceover. It was empty.

"Why didn't you say something?"

"I'm terrified, man. Everyone just started going crazy when that message came on the television. I heard all sorts of shouting, and banging, I think I even heard a gunshot at one point. I don't know what's going on, man, and I have no idea what to do. When I heard footsteps coming up the stairs I hid, until I heard your door open, and realised you'd come back. I figured that we've known each other for ages now, and you've always been decent to me, so I would take a chance and come see if maybe you had a plan that I could help with."

"We know about the same as you do, Br-"

"We?"

"Shit, sorry, Beck, it's alright, you can come out."

Beck appeared from the restroom, still holding the knife in her right hand.

"Whoa, man, listen, I'm not going to be any trouble for you," he was looking directly at the knife.

"Would you put that thing away, please?" I asked Beck.

"How do we know we can trust him? How do we know he isn't going to try to take our supplies?" her hand was shaking, but she wasn't putting that knife down. Her knuckles were white from the force of her grip. Beck didn't look at me once, she just stared straight at Brad. He put his hands up slowly, sweat began to form on his forehead.

"Beck, I know him. Believe me, Brad is harmless."

"They say that serial killers are the last people you expect, Cole, just how sure are you about your neighbour?"

"I'm sure! 100% sure. I am just going to need you to trust me. We need him, every extra person we have gives us more of a chance of figuring out what's going on here, and what we're going to do about it. Now, please, put the knife down."

She stared straight at Brad.

"If I suspect something funny, even just for a second, I won't hesitate to protect us," she walked to the bag, placing the knife directly on top of everything, not zipping it shut. She sat on the bed, right next to the bag.

"The bag stays with me. Any problems?" she looked at me for the first time.

"No," I said defensively.

Brad dropped his hands, the sweat from his forehead had formed a wet patch on the carpet by his feet. I got kitchen towels and handed them to him. He dabbed at his forehead.

"Thanks, man."

"No problem."

"So, what do we do now?" Beck asked.

"What food do you have at your place, Brad?"

"Not too sure, I'll go get it all and bring it here so we can see."

"No, you won't," Beck stood up, picking up the knife once more. "I'll go get the food. What number are you in?"

The Cost of Good Intentions

"Okay then, number 7, can you just make sure you bring my weed as well? My anxiety has flared up after all this."

Beck scoffed as she left the room.

She came back 15 minutes later with 2 big grocery bags. They were bulging, they looked so heavy that the straps might break.

She dropped them at her feet as soon as she got through the door, some of the contents spilled onto the floor. Her face was red, her hair was matted and sticking to her forehead.

Finally, the first bit of luck.

"How much food do you keep at home? There are 3 more bags down the stairs," she panted.

"Listen, man, don't judge me. The munchies have no preferences."

I stifled a laugh and went to go get the remaining bags.

I was a bit less pleased when I saw what the bags contained.

There were 10 bags of microwave rice. 4 portions of microwave macaroni and cheese. 4 microwave bacon and cheeseburgers. 2 loaves of bread. A few cans of baked beans, and about a kilogram of sweets and chocolate.

This food along with the food in my apartment wouldn't even get us through the week.

It just confirmed that we would have to do the one thing I was dreading.

"Cole, your hands are shaking."

I needed a drink. I grabbed my left wrist with my right hand, pretending to massage the joint.

The Cost of Good Intentions

"We are going to need to try get to a Super-market. These supplies aren't going to last us long at all. If we are going to go out there, each of us is going to need a weapon."

"No way, I'm not letting him anywhere near something he could use against us, Cole."

"What choice do we have? Honestly Beck, right now we aren't in any position that grants the luxury of a choice like that. We all need to be able to protect ourselves, and each other."

"It's just that in all the time that I've known you, you've never once told me about Brad, Cole. How much time have you actually spent together?"

Brad intervened, "In all the time that I've known Cole, he's never mentioned you either."

"Look, we're just going to have to trust each other, okay. I don't want to hear any more about it."

"Fine," Beck whispered, barely enough for anyone to hear.

"Good, now let's get ready."

I opened the kitchen drawer, handing a knife to Brad, and taking one for myself.

I stared at the blade for a moment. I couldn't believe that it was just yesterday that I was worried about losing my job, and now that wasn't even a problem.

I put the knife in the back of my trousers. The blade was cold against my skin. I tried walking, making sure that it wasn't going to hurt me in the process. It all seemed fine.

Brad copied my idea,

"Ready?" I asked

Beck replied, looking straight at the door.

"Do we have a choice?"

CHAPTER 5

While Beck and I packed the food into the cupboards, Brad rolled up and smoked a joint in the restroom. I had a glass of vodka to stop my hands from shaking. Brad came out the restroom, his eyes looked like someone had taken a red crayon and coloured over all the white that surrounded his blue iris.
"That's better."
"I can't believe the two of you, we need to be sharp."
"I am more focused when I'm stoned, okay."
"If you say so."
"Let's get going."
We headed for the door, I switched off the light on the way out. When we were all out, I locked the door, and put the keys in my jacket pocket.
We walked down the stairs, careful not to make too much noise.
There were 3 apartments on my level, with 2 on each level below. While we walked down I counted 3 lights on. I contemplated trying one of the doors to see if there was anyone else here but decided against it. Brad was the only person I spoke to in the entire building, and from what he described earlier, I wasn't sure it was a good time to try make friends with the neighbours.
We reached the street, each of us pulled our hoods over our heads in turn as a cold breeze made its presence known.
"Where are we headed, Cole?"
"The Super-market is 3 miles away."

The Cost of Good Intentions

We walked at a good pace, carefully looking for anything that looked out of the ordinary. It was hard not to panic. Anyone could be hiding, anywhere. The only comforting thing was that we didn't have anything of any value. All we had were clothes in the bag, but then again, people have been killed for less.

I tried not to think about it too much.

We turned the corner onto St. Vincent Street. The street was, like all the others, deserted. Cars were parked on either side of the street.

My mind began to drift, taking me back to the day that I met Elon.

Both my parents were lawyers for various celebrities, so we moved around, a lot.

The first time we moved I was 8, I had just made my first friend, Marcus. I got home from school that day, I brought Marcus with so we could play. When I opened the door, I saw taped up cardboard boxes all over. They were stacked up on top of each other in piles that reached the ceiling.

My parents were in their room, elbow deep in boxes. My mother spotted me just as she was packing a set of bed sheets into a box marked, "Mom and Dad bedroom."

Once they saw the two of us, I didn't even get a chance to introduce Marcus.

My father took Marcus back to his house, and the next day we were on the road, heading to what would be my 2nd of 7 schools.

We moved round so much that I never got a chance to make any friends. Every time I came remotely close to having anything that even resembled a friend we moved. I used to feel like they did it as some sort of sick punishment for something I had done. I used to spend days thinking what it was I had done, trying to be better, trying not to do it again so that we wouldn't have to move again. I understand now that it had nothing to do with what I had done, and everything to do with priorities. In those days, the days of what would become known as, "the Before Times", we had to choose whether we wanted to live comfortably or live happily. I suppose we still did at the time the sun disappeared.

By the time I met Elon, I had completely given up on making friends. I found comfort in my art and never got too involved in anything else, but sometimes life has other plans for us.

I met Elon on a warm summer day, on this very street. I had just moved to the neighbourhood, and I was taking a walk around, trying to familiarise myself with everything.

A lone skateboard was coming in my direction. I stood on top of it to stop it when it got close enough. I bent down to pick it up. Moments later a tall boy with lots of freckles was standing in front of me.

"Give me back my skateboard. Fucker."

"I... I...No problem, here," I held out the board, waiting for him to take it from me.

He kicked me straight below my knee, instead. The pain was excruciating, he had hit me right between the bone and cartilage. I dropped the board, clutching at my knee, trying not to vomit from the pain.

"Pick it up."

I didn't know what that kid's problem was, but I wasn't going to ask questions. I let go of my aching knee, picking up his board. I tried to give it to him, again, this time he took it.

"Next time, don't try steal my board."

I turned around to walk back home. There was a tall boy with slick black hair standing in front of me, now. He wore a black leather jacket, with a white shirt. A silver watch dangled from his left wrist. It was Elon.

"How's about you apologise to my friend, Paul."

"Your friend tried to steal my board, we've sorted it out though, unless you and I have a problem, Gatner?"

"We do have a problem if you don't apologise," Elon passed me and walked towards Paul; they were roughly the same height. Neither of them flinched as they both stared each other right in the eye.

"I'm giving you to 3 to get out of my face, Gatner."

"Do you want me to count for you?"

Paul punched Elon straight in the nose. Elon was on the floor in less than a second, blood streaming from his nose. Despite this, Elon smiled straight up at Paul, blood staining his teeth now.

"Run along now, you've made your point."

"You're pathetic, Gatner."

Paul picked up his board, turned, and was on his way.

I ran over to Elon. I extended my hand when I got to him, he took it, and I pulled him up.

"Put your head back, you don't want to lose too much blood."

"Are you a doctor or something?" he smiled as he tilted his head back.

The Cost of Good Intentions

"Do you know where the nearest store is, I can get you some tissue so you can plug your nose. I just don't know where anything is, I am new here."

"Clearly, otherwise you wouldn't have touched Paul's skateboard," another smile. "There is a Super-Market just down the street, to the right."

We walked to the Super-Market; Elon waited outside while I went inside. I bought tissues and two iced creams. Elon was waiting for me on a bench that was in the shade, in the parking lot. I handed him the tissues and an iced cream before sitting down next to him. He opened the tissues first, twisting the ends of two of them and shoving one into each nostril.

"What's with the iced cream?"

"Just saying thank you, if you don't want it, I can take it back."

"No, no. I'll take it, the sun is hot today."

"True."

"So, where you from...uhm…"

"Cole, Cole Clay."

"So, where you from, Cole Clay?"

"Just Cole, and you know, here and there. Everywhere."

"Must be nice, that's where my dad is from."

"Is he a lawyer, too?"

"Yeah, something like that."

Both tissues were stained scarlet red with blood. Elon changed them out for fresh ones.

"You should get that checked out; I think he might have broken your nose."

"Wouldn't be the first time."

The Cost of Good Intentions

"He's broken your nose before?"

"Not him, particularly, but at least 4 people have broken my nose. I thought you could tell, I mean, look at it," he turned and faced me. He was right, his nose was extremely skew.

"It isn't really noticeable," I lied, "Did you really think you could take Paul on?"

"Never."

"Then why did you do it?"

"Listen, Cole. If you show people that it's okay to fuck with you, they're going to keep doing it. The moment you stand up for yourself, they give you something, do you know what that something is?"

"No."

"It's called respect, Cole. The way I see it, Paul is like a one trick pony, and once you take away that trick, he doesn't have anything else. Once he realizes he can't physically hurt you, he'll move on to someone he can."

"I never thought about it like that before."

"Stick with me, kid. I'll keep you straight."

Beck, Brad and I stood outside the Super-Market. I stared at that bench and wondered where Elon was. I didn't even know where to start looking for him. I couldn't think about that now.

The parking lot was completely empty. We approached the building, there weren't too many trolleys left. The ones that were still there were all over the place, the small metal chain that linked them had been broken on each one. I tried to look into the building, to see if there was anyone inside, but some of the aisles were out of our view.

"Cole, look," Brad was pointing towards a hole in the glass exterior of the building.

"Okay, listen. When we go in there we're going to need to split up, so that if anyone is in there, we have a chance of getting to them before they can run and possibly get more people who could hurt us."

"What are we supposed to do if we find someone?" Beck looked concerned.

"If anyone comes across someone else, run to the next aisle and throw something high into the air. The other two will then come and help. We will need to restrain them, just until we can establish if they're a threat or not."

Beck was visibly panicking at the thought.

"What if we don't find anyone?" Brad asked

"There is a giant clock on the wall at the back, when we enter, check the time. We have 10 minutes to look. If you don't find anyone in the 10 minutes, then meet back out here.

"What the fuck is going on here. I can't even believe that we just had that discussion. I don't know, Cole. I don't know if I can do it," Beck was having another full-blown meltdown.

"You had no problem threatening me a couple of hours ago," Brad interrupted

"I didn't have time to think about that, did I?" She practically screamed.

"Oh well, there goes our element of surprise, good job."

"Can the two of you both stop having a go at each other, it isn't going to help anyone," I harshly whispered.

"It's her."

The Cost of Good Intentions

"It's him."

"Both of you, enough! We need to go in and see what we can get. I'll take the first 5 aisles, Beck, you take the middle 5, Brad, you take the last 5, alright?"

"Alright," they both mumbled.

We approached the building. Beck put the bag with all our emergency clothing in a bush to the side of the building.

I went first, careful to avoid the jagged edges of the glass. I waited to make sure that Beck and Brad made it inside alright. When they did, I pointed at the clock. It was 21:25. We split up.

The lights were bright, we were going to have to try use the shelves as cover, so we weren't spotted. I was crouched down, trying to control my breathing as I approached the first aisle. I placed my back on the shelf and reached for my knife, gripping the handle firmly.

My heart was racing as I peeked out into the first aisle. It was empty. I stayed crouched as I slowly made my way through the aisle. I was careful not to make a sound as I looked at the shelves. Some sections had already been emptied, but there was still a decent number of things that would help us.

I got to the end of the aisle and carefully positioned myself with my back against the second shelf. Empty again. I repeated my process, until I was sure that nobody else was here.

I looked at the clock, 21:33. I carefully made my way back outside.

Beck and Brad came shortly after me. We were alone.

I grabbed a trolley and pushed it through the hole. The edges scraped the sides of the trolley as we went in.

The Cost of Good Intentions

I immediately made my way to the alcohol section. I was in heaven, knowing that I didn't have to pay for a single thing.

"Not too much, we need space for things that we actually need to survive," Beck was walking toward the canned food section. Brad went for the electronics section.

I picked up a few bottles of the most expensive vodka they had on the shelves, I opened a bottle and took a sip as I pushed the trolley toward the aisle that had instant noodles.

I took as many as my arms could grab and dropped them into the trolley. I went to find Beck. She put a selection of tinned soups, beans, carrots and tomatoes into the trolley.

"Who knew the end of the world would force me to diet?"

"Well, we can't take a lot of fresh food, they'll go off too quickly, Cole."

"I know, I know."

We walked over to the crisps section and threw in what they had left.

Brad came to us; he was struggling to hold a pile of batteries. He let them fall in the trolley when he was in range, he then reached into his pocket and pulled out 3 torches.

"We're going to need these if the power goes out. There are also some battery-operated heaters, we're going to need those too."

We went and got the heaters. The trolley was almost full, so we decided that we had enough for the time being.

We walked out, Beck grabbed the bag from the bush, and we started walking back to my apartment.

The Cost of Good Intentions

We were back on St. Vincent Street when I stopped. The car door of a blue Ford Focus was open. I could see a person's feet when I looked to the space beneath the open door. Someone was hunched over, into the car, searching for something. Beck and Brad, both saw him as well. We looked at each other before silently deciding it was best to retreat and try another route back, but it was too late. The person knew we were there. He emerged from the car, putting his hands in front of him.

"Hey. Hey! Do you guys know what's going on? I can't find anyone. My cell is dead, and I can't find my charger. What's happened to the sun?" he moved out from behind the car door, keeping his hands in front of him. His eyes drifted to the trolley for the briefest of moments.

Beck reached for her knife, dropping the bag with the clothing in the process. Her hand gripped the handle of the knife, but she didn't pull it out.

"Whoa… Believe me, I'm not here to hurt you, I really am harmless."

Brad clenched his fists at his side but said nothing.

"What's your name?"

"My name… my name is Rory."

"Okay, Rory, I am going to need you to slowly empty your pockets. If they are already empty pull the insides out, so we can see."

"S…Sure. N…No problem."

He exposed all of his pockets; they were all empty.

"Where's your phone?"

"I keep it in my sock, so nobody will find it if they try and rob me."

"Take it out and put it on the ground."

The Cost of Good Intentions

He slowly started to squat, bringing his right hand down, while his left hand remained above his head.

"Cole, I don't like this, man," Brad said.

It all happened so quickly. Rory's right hand made it into his left sock, and instead of his phone, he pulled out a pistol.

Beck pulled out her knife.

He quickly fired in my direction. I managed to move, just in time, to avoid a bullet headed straight for my stomach. Two more shots, and one caught Beck's leg. She screamed in agony as she fell to the ground.

I rushed forward and pushed the trolley with all my force towards Rory. He moved out of the way, into the middle of the street. His focus was on dodging the trolley, which gave me enough time to get close enough to tackle him. The gun flew from his grip as we both fell to the ground. He quickly did a roll that put him on top. I put my hands up, and covered my head just in time to block a blow headed straight for my face. I shifted my body weight and tried to flip us over again. I was unsuccessful, he was able to pin my arms to my sides with his knees. There wasn't anything I could do to stop him. He hit me three times, hard. Before he could land a fourth blow Brad tackled him off me. Rory used the momentum from the tackle and got Brad into the same position he had me in a moment before. I scrambled to my feet; he would kill him if I didn't do something. I ran as fast as my legs would allow, drawing my knife from the back of my trousers. I reached them, before thinking about anything.

I stabbed Rory.

The Cost of Good Intentions

The knife was stuck in his ribs as he collapsed onto his side.

I watched as he gripped the handle and pulled the knife from his body.

Blood squirted from the wound as the knife came free. Rory screamed in agony as he put his hand over the fresh wound.

I was frozen. Frozen in this moment, looking at this man bleed to death.

I did this.

Brad got up and ran to me. He stood in front of me, blocking my view of the gruesome scene. His face was bloody, a black eye was already forming. His blonde hair was stained with blood. I had a feeling I didn't look too much better.

"Don't watch, man," he took my wrist and ushered me towards Beck. I didn't feel like any of it was real. I felt like I was in another person's body, watching from the outside in.

Beck was on the floor, putting pressure onto the bullet wound in her leg. She let out a few exasperated screams, tears were freely flowing down her cheeks.

"Cole, he shot me." she began to wail, "It's so sore, Cole."

I couldn't say anything, I was in shock. I just walked over, kneeling next to her, and took her hand. She squeezed it tightly as she cried.

"We need to get out of here. We're going to need to put Beck into the trolley and wheel her back," Brad was already moving toward the trolley; it was lying on its side halfway down the street. Most of the contents had spilled onto the street, the cans of vegetables had burst, but all the alcohol was surprisingly intact. Brad saved what he could, putting everything that was still okay into the bag with the clothing, before he pushed the trolley over.

"I'm going to need your help lifting her into the trolley, Cole."

"Okay," I mumbled.

Beck put one hand on my shoulder, and one hand on Brad's. Brad and I locked each other's hands underneath her legs and lifted, gently. We tried our best to not disturb the wound, which was plugged by the bullet, as we gently placed her into the trolley.

"Let's get back to the apartment."

Brad pushed the trolley; I picked up the bag. I looked back at Rory, he was looking up at the sky, his breathing shallow.

"Please, it's so sore. Please, just kill me," he gasped for air.

I turned; we walked away.

CHAPTER 6

We got back to the apartment without any more issues. I got the keys from my pocket and dropped the bag so that I could help Brad lift Beck. We carried her up the stairs, once we were at the top the both of us were out of breath. I strained as I tried to unlock the door. I pushed the door open once I was successful, and we angled ourselves into the room before we carefully placed Beck onto the bed. The pain had subsided for the time being. She had a cold sweat running across her forehead, her eyes were blank as she looked up at the ceiling. Brad ran down and fetched the bag, before returning a moment later.

"Give me some scissors, Cole."

"What do y-"

"Just give me scissors!" she screamed.

I got some scissors from the kitchen drawer and handed them to her. She carefully cut her jeans up, exposing the bullet hole. The skin around the wound was filled with dry blood as fresh blood leaked from the small gaps around the bullet. I looked at Brad as he put the bag down on the side of the bed.

"What do we do now? We can't get her to a hospital, and we can't leave that bullet in there."

"I've watched tons of videos about this, man. I can do it."

"Yeah, because that fills me with a ton of confidence, having a stoner pull a bullet from my leg after watching a YouTube tutorial. Hurray, I am saved," Beck said, sarcastically.

"Listen, you've done nothing but be rude ever since I got here. I could have run with everything when you were down with a bullet in your leg, and Cole was getting beat by Rory, but I didn't. Now unless you have a doctor, hiding in the cupboard, that can extract this bullet, I suggest you keep quiet."

"Okay, no need to throw your toys out the cot."

"I'm going to get materials."

He went to his apartment and came back, his eyes freshly red, with a full sewing kit. He had a box with all kinds of thread, each compartment in the box was neatly labelled. He pulled out a string of nylon thread and tied a neat knot into the eye of the needle, before he lit a candle and placed it beside him.

"Okay Cole, I need some alcohol to dab the wound."

I handed him a bottle of vodka from the bag. He took a bit of cloth from his pocket and poured some of the vodka into the cloth.

"This is going to burn; you might want to bite onto this," he handed her a cloth from his other pocket. Beck took the bottle from me and took a huge gulp before she took the cloth and bit down onto it.

Brad took a pair of tweezers from the kit.

"Cole, I am going to need you to put your hand around the wound and pull outwards, gently, so I can grip the bullet cleanly."

I followed his instruction. I could feel Beck's leg muscle tense as I opened the wound. A small stream of blood dribbled from the hole. Brad's hand was extremely steady as he slowly gripped the edges of the bullet with his pair of

The Cost of Good Intentions

tweezers. He exhaled; a bead of sweat was running down his nose as he intensely focused on the job at hand.

He slowly pulled the bullet, careful not to lose his grip. Beck bit down onto the cloth, she screamed, but the sound was muffled. When the bullet was almost out, he gave a final sharp tug. Blood flowed from the wound, without rest. I stopped forcing it open.

He placed the bullet on a saucer next to him and picked up the needle that had the thread.

He heated it with the candle before he expertly started to stitch the wound closed. Criss-crossing the thread as the blood stopped. He cut the thread and tied a knot into the ends.

"Holy shit! You did it! You actually did it!"

Beck pulled the cloth from her mouth. Her face was red from the pain, her hair plastered to her forehead. Brad took the saucer with the bullet, disposing of it into the bin, along with the needle. He closed his kit and placed it onto the bed beside my right leg, and then he blew the candle out.

"I'm not sure when you're going to be able to walk on it, but you should rest for a bit."

"I never thought I would say this, but, thank you Brad."

"Don't mention it, man."

CHAPTER 7

AMELIA

I hate hospitals. I was 9 years old when I first came with my dad to one. That day changed everything. The sky was full of dark clouds that looked ready to burst. A few rays of sunlight broke through a small gap in the clouds on the horizon. I looked at them, the perfect vertical slants illuminated tiny spots of open land, breaking up the morbidity that was life in Nod.

We cruised along a long and, seemingly, never-ending road in our half-broken Kia Picanto.

What a wonderful world by Louis Armstrong was blaring through the speakers.

It was dad's 4th hospital visit in as many weeks. If he was nervous he didn't show it.

A few drops of rain gently hit the windscreen moments before we found ourselves in full on showers. Before we got to the hospital the rain stopped and we were engulfed in the sun's magnificent incandescence.

Dad parked the car when we got to the hospital. The black smoke coming from the exhaust ceased as he turned the key to stop the engine. I always used to get nervous when he turned that engine off, because I was never completely sure that it was going to come on again. My dad got out the car and came around to my side. He opened my door and undid my seatbelt.

"Come now, Amelia. I'm supposed to see the doctor in 10 minutes," he held out his hand for me to take, I took it. He pulled me up out of my seat with little to no effort, now holding me in his arms. I giggled as he kissed my cheek. "Daaaad, stop, you're embarrassing me!" I smiled at him. He put me down and shut my door. I took his hand as we walked toward the hospital. The building was huge, white walls towered high as I craned my neck backwards. There were hundreds of windows, each one was open. The building looked really clean from the outside, but when we walked through the rotating doors I knew this wasn't a place you wanted to be. Hospitals are a bit like people in that sense. Some of them are really nice to look at from the outside, but the deeper you go inside, the more fucked up it becomes.

It wasn't like there were people being rushed on gurneys everywhere, blood seeping out of fresh wounds. There weren't even people screaming from being in excruciating pain. No. Hospitals are much worse than that. You walk in and just look at the people, some stare mindlessly at the television on the wall, not even registering what they're seeing. Some stare at their clasped together hands, deep in thought. Some people look up when they hear a door open, a light flickering in their eyes as they wait anxiously for the doctor to give them whatever verdict they're waiting for.

Nearly all of them look broken, in one way or another, and not the kind of broken that can be fixed in a couple of days.

"Hi, I am here to see Dr Richards."

"What's your name?"

"Ben Clark."

The Cost of Good Intentions

"Okay Mr Clark, take a seat and the doctor will be with you in a couple of minutes."

"Thank you, ma'am."

We left reception and went to the waiting area, sitting on two plastic seats in the far corner of the room, my dad helped me up to my seat. I looked up at the TV. They were playing an old episode of the Simpsons. I didn't get a chance to even grasp what the episode was about before the doctor called my dad.

"Mr Clark."

"Yes, sir."

"If you'll follow me, please."

We got up and walked towards the man in the white coat.

"I'm Dr Richards, if you'll follow me, my office is just down the hall."

He didn't look like the doctors from TV. For one, he was shorter than my dad, who wasn't the tallest man around. He was also going bald on the top of his head, that exact spot glistened every time we walked under a light in the corridor. He had ugly glasses and wrinkles, while the doctors on TV were always tall, dark and handsome.

Dr Richards opened a door in the middle of the corridor and ushered us inside.

He waited until we were both inside before closing the door behind us. There was a big wooden table in the centre of the room with one rotating leather chair on one side and two plastic chairs on the other side. Framed certificates lined the walls of the office, including a master's degree from Oxford University. A flat screen computer was in the corner of the desk, sitting next to the keyboard was a half-eaten apple. I found that quite ironic.

The Cost of Good Intentions

"Please, have a seat."

"Thank you, sir," my dad said as he helped me into my seat before he settled into his. Dr Richards sat in his chair and began flicking through some notes. It didn't take long before he removed his glasses and placed them neatly onto the table. He looked at my dad, a look of sadness washed over his face.

It felt like an eternity before he looked at me and smiled.

"We have some sweets in the reception, sweetheart, would you like me to get a nurse to help you get some?"

"Yes, please! Yes!" I was already out of my seat, itching for some sugar.

"No, sir. Whatever you can tell me, you can tell her as well."

I looked at my dad, he had a stern look on his face.

"Are you sure, Mr Clark?"

"I am," he tapped the chair next to him as he looked at me, "sit down, Amelia, the doctor has some news for us."

"But, sweets daddy," I whined

"We can get the sweets later, now sit."

He never spoke to me like that, I could tell that something wasn't right. I stopped jumping around and sat down.

"The test results are back, Mr Clark."

"How bad?"

"Stage 3 leukaemia."

"Thank you for letting me know Dr Richards. We'll be on our way now."

"Mr Clark, I must insist on treatment if you have any chance of beating this."

"Thank you for your time, sir."

My dad stood up quickly and gestured for me to take his hand. I took it and we headed for the exit.

Dr Richards was jogging after us and just as we were about to reach reception he managed to catch up.

"Look, Ben, just take a leaflet. I can't force you in to anything but given your circumstances I would strongly suggest you at least try to fight this. If not for yourself, do it for your daughter."

My dad looked Dr Richards in the eye and took the leaflet.

Dr Richards started walking back to his office and we started walking for the exit.

We got into the car and my dad pulled out a CD from the glove compartment before starting the car.

We started our journey home, black smoke bellowing from the rusty exhaust as Stand by Me from Ben E. King softly played in the background when my dad threw the pamphlet out the window.

"Amy, wake up," Rory had his hand on my shoulders and was shaking me.

I groggily opened my eyes and waited for my vision to clear, I sat up and began rubbing the sleep away from my eyes.

"Rory, it's the middle of the night, we'll go to Super-Market in the morning."

"That's just it, it's not the middle of the night, it's 8 o'clock, Amy."

"Well, that can't be true, the sun's still not up and it's the middle of summer."

"I know that! That's why I'm waking you up, genius."

The Cost of Good Intentions

"Okay, Rory, ha ha. You got me."

He handed me the clock. The screen was cracked, and it was quite an old clock, but it still worked, the seconds hand was still ticking.

Initially I just thought that Rory was playing one of his stupid jokes on me. He had been moaning for a while that he was hungry and kept saying we should go check the dumpsters behind the Super-Market to see if they had thrown anything out.

"So, when did you change it?"

"Oh my God, Amy, this isn't a joke. I didn't touch the clock."

I was starting to get annoyed. Rory could be a bit too much at times, he never really had a limit. This one time he told me that the new manager at the clothes store around the corner was his best friend in high school, and that he had negotiated that we could each take an outfit for free, because the guy felt sorry for him. He even started speaking to the guy while I was in the store, he disappeared somewhere while I was browsing. It wasn't until I was at the till, talking to the cashier about Rory's deal with the manager that I realized that he had actually left the store and it was all a giant joke. I met him outside the store, he was howling with laughter, but that was just Rory. He was my only friend in this world.

So, when he told me about the clock, I didn't believe him, but I knew better at this point than to not play along when he got into one of these moods. If I didn't, he would sulk, and not just for a couple of hours, I mean days, and that would be far worse than the half mile walk to the Super-Market.

I got out my sleeping bag, folded it up, and put it into my backpack. Rory did the same before grabbing the clock and stuffing it into the front compartment of his bag. I watched as he rolled up his trousers over his left ankle and pulled out his pistol. He opened the chamber to take an inventory on how much ammo he had. This was the norm, but I noticed his hands were shaking a little today. It was strange as it had been a while since I had seen him nervous to hold the gun. We never had to use it, but both of us agreed it was necessary, after all we had been jumped a few times in the years we had been homeless. We got the gun about 5 years ago after another homeless man tried to steal my bag. We were camped underneath a bridge, much like that day, Rory had gone to beg outside a bar around the corner. He'd been doing it late in the night so when these drunk guys used to walk out, they would either give him some money or want to beat him up, because the alcohol brought out the extremes in them. In the case that they wanted to beat him up, he just used to lie about what one drunk guy said about another drunk guy's wife and it would end up in these huge brawls where lots of people would get knocked out and Rory would just be there taking their wallets and whatever jewellery that had on them. I didn't condone of stealing or take part in it, but at points it was that money that helped us buy an extra layer of clothing when it was colder than normal, or a bit of food when the bins had been raided before we got there.

This homeless man saw where we had been camping and noticed that I was alone a lot in the evenings so one night he came and pointed his pistol at me and told me to give him all our belongings. I was slowly gathering our things; the man was sweating so much, and he looked genuinely upset that it had come to this. I was just about to hand him the bag when Rory came back early. The police had wanted to arrest him after they realized that he was the one starting all the fights. When Rory saw the man pointing the pistol at me he quickly realized what was going on and tackled the stranger from behind. Rory was a strong man, even if he didn't look it. He constantly exercised, and when we did buy food, it was always healthy. The gun flew in the air and landed right at my feet. I picked it up and pointed it straight at the stranger, before I told him to leave.

We packed our stuff and left that evening and made our way to the bridge we slept under on the day that the sun went missing.

When we first got the gun Rory would practice assembling it, loading it, and occasionally we would go to this open field about 2 miles away so he could practice shooting at a few cans we would collect from the bins. His forehead would glisten with sweat as he focussed on hitting his targets. The few times someone has tried to rob us since then, Rory just pulled the gun out and they ran away. So, it became easier, knowing that he never really had to shoot anyone, and we got to keep our things.

I didn't know why his hands were shaking, but I didn't like it.

CHAPTER 8

We started our walk to Super-Market, and it didn't take long for a strange feeling to creep into my stomach as I noticed the lack of movement around. I didn't see any people, or cars moving, or much of anything really. The streets were all flooded from the rain the night before. There was a huge storm, but the bridge we camped under was low and covered us quite well. Every second or third house light was on, and all the streetlights were on as well. I tried not to pay attention to it. I tried to focus, like I had done for years. Zone out all that isn't important and just focus on the goal, at that time the goal had been to reach Super-Market, so that's what I did, and we made it.

When we reached the car park it was completely empty. Rory ran to the outskirts of a parking lot and came back with a brick. He was just about to throw it straight at the window when I grabbed his wrist.

"What are you doing? Are you crazy? The alarm will go off and they will catch and arrest us!"

"Who? Who is going to arrest us, Amy? Look around, there is nobody here, and we need the supplies for whatever is going on."

"Going on!?" I had lost it at that point, "What's going on is you're trying to break into a place and try to play it off as some kind of joke, Rory!"

"This isn't a joke!" he had a crazy look in his eyes.

"Typical Rory, never knowing when to stop! It's enough! It isn't funny, and it never was! Just change the clock back and let's go back home, back to bed."

"I didn't change the clock! Why would I ever do that?"

"I don't understand why you do a lot of things."

The Cost of Good Intentions

"Amy, look at me," he grabbed both my shoulders. I tried to pull away and start walking back but his grip was firm. "I didn't change the clock. The sun is gone. It is 8:30 and I have no idea where anyone is. I am not joking, we need the supplies, and we need to figure out what is going on."

I realized the severity of the situation we were in. This was not a joke, or some nonsensical ploy to feed into Rory's eternal boredom. This was real. We were in danger.

I took the brick from him and dropped it onto the floor beside my left foot.

"I'm telling the fucking truth, Amy!" his eyes were wild, little spit droplets flung from his mouth as he practically spat the words at me.

I walked over to the trolleys and pulled one free from the others, before pointing it directly at the exterior of the building.

Rory was silent, now, as he watched me take a small run up before pushing the trolley with all my might towards the building.

The glass shattered, creating a hole that we could use to gain entry into the store. The alarm sounded as soon as the trolley penetrated the glass, the siren would attract anyone within a mile radius.

"I believe you," I shouted as I started walking towards the newly formed hole.

"We need to be quick, just grab essentials and let's get out of here before anyone decides to look what is going on."

We both headed into the building. The sound from the alarm was deafening inside so we had to cover our ears as we weaved our way in and out of aisles looking for earplugs before we started the process of slowly filling the trolley with a large number of tinned foods, multipacks of water bottles and a few warm cotton blankets. We were so used to surviving off of the bare minimum that this process didn't even take any thought, we both knew exactly what we needed to survive. This entire situation had actually worked out in our favour, because on this occasion we didn't need to worry about paying for anything. As we grabbed the last of our usual supplies and made our way back toward the hole, Rory suddenly stopped walking.

He was saying something, but I couldn't hear him at all. Conveniently we were in the aisle with stationary. I picked up a bag of pens and a notebook and handed them to Rory.

He took both and started writing something on the first page. When he was finished, he handed it to me to read.

"We need to go to the office to see if we can erase the camera footage."

I hadn't thought about that, and when I did, I realised that, technically speaking, we *had* just stolen from a store. I didn't like the thought, so I blocked it out from my mind before I turned to Rory.

"Okay," I mouthed before looking to see where the office might be.

I spotted a black door right at the back of the store that looked like it would lead to a staff area. Rory saw it at the same time as I did and we both began walking towards it, Rory in front while I followed with the trolley. The door had a blue sign stating, "no unauthorized access" which was placed firmly in the centre. We made our way through. On the other side was a long corridor. There were two doors on the left, two on the right, and a double door right at the end of the corridor with a red siren illuminated. The first door on the left had a sign indicating that it was the staff room. The two doors on the right were the toilets. Which meant that the second door on the left would have to be the manager's office. I left the trolley outside and we entered the office.

The lights were on, but it was still dark in the room. Another siren was flashing red in the top corner above the door. There was a computer on a wooden desk, with multiple drawers, in front of a chair with wheels. In a corner, underneath the desk was a steel safe with a keypad on the door.

Rory walked to the computer and moved the mouse around. The screen illuminated to display a green grassy field. There were so many files on the screen, it was almost filled entirely with the little file icons. I watched as Rory moved the mouse over each, expanding the text, when necessary, until he found the file he was looking for.

There it was in the middle of the third row.

"Security Cam Footage."

He clicked on the icon and the screen changed to a page with the dreaded word, "Password" clearly written above a box with a blinking cursor. I was just about to tap his arm and motion for us to leave while we still could when I saw him step away from the PC and start rummaging through the drawers.

At the bottom of a pile of papers was a notebook.

Rory pulled the notebook out of the drawer and started reading its contents. He must have found what he was looking for, because he moved back to the PC and input.

"Cameras123!"

The screen changed again. It was now filled with around 15 different views of the store. He clicked on an arrow in the top corner and a menu opened. There was a section called, "footage" and when he moved the cursor over to it, a sub menu opened with the word, "delete" in it.

The Cost of Good Intentions

He clicked on it and selected, "present day" from the options. The screen refreshed with more new text asking for a password, once again. Rory flicked through the book again before settling on a new page.

He then entered, "Boss213!" and a new message popped up saying that the footage had been successfully deleted. He looked at me and smiled. I smiled back before he started walking with the notebook towards a keypad on the wall. He entered 1324 into the keypad and everything went silent. The sirens weren't illuminated anymore.

I took out my earplugs and Rory did the same.

"How did you know how to do that!? That was amazing! You are like a computer genius!" I struggled to keep the amazement out of my voice.

"I was a manager at a place like this, once."

"Really? How come you never told me?" I asked, still smiling broadly.

"It didn't really seem important until now, I suppose."

"Well, that was amazing, Rory."

"Thanks," he was blushing, ever so slightly.

I felt sad as I realized I didn't ever really compliment Rory. He did incredible things every day, that I got used to over all the years. I don't know what I would have done if he wasn't around, not just that day, but every day since we had met each other. There were cold nights where he had seen me shivering. I would wake up the next morning with his blanket on top of mine, while he slept without one. He never expected anything in return, either, and he didn't do it as a romantic gesture that he would cash in on later. That wasn't in Rory's nature.

To him, I paid him back with my company; I paid him back by staying when everyone else had left.

The Cost of Good Intentions

I stared at him and noticed, for the first time, just how weathered he looked. His skin was not wrinkly, but it was hard. The bags under his eyes were so naturally black that you could argue he used make-up. The creases on his forehead had gained a sharp edge to them, and his dark hair looked frazzled as it threatened to begin the process of turning grey. His eyes were creased at the sides from the smile he wore so proudly after his heroics just a few moments ago.

"You go get the trolley; I'm just going to put everything back where it was before we go."

"Okay, Rory," I smiled as I walked toward the door.

Once I was in the corridor, I grabbed the trolley handles and began pushing the trolley to the emergency exit at the end of the corridor. I hadn't even pushed it two steps when I heard voices.

They were feint but after a few seconds I could clearly tell that they were getting louder. I didn't know how many there were, the trolley couldn't fit inside the tiny manager's office. I needed to think, and fast.

I abandoned the trolley and headed back to the manager's office to fetch Rory. I would be safe there; Rory had the gun. I did my best to keep my footsteps as silent as possible and when I opened the door I did it so carefully that even Rory didn't hear me enter.

At least that's what I thought.

He didn't hear me because, when I entered the office, I saw him elbow deep inside the safe. At least half a dozen plastic bags were on the floor. His pockets were bulging with money. My mind was racing with anger, and panic, taking over all my senses. I rushed over to him, continuing to hear the voices getting louder and louder. His eye caught mine as he turned around when he eventually heard me approach. He looked remorseful, but that conversation would have to wait.

"There are people in here," I whispered, frantically.

I saw him start to panic.

"Quick, get in, I will let you out when they are gone," he was gesturing towards the newly empty safe.

I didn't like it, but I didn't have much of a choice at this point, so I climbed in. I hugged my legs close to my chest and just about managed to fit into the safe. Rory closed the door, and I watched as the little light that was present in the office got consumed by darkness.

I could hear my shallow breathing as I held back sobs.

How had it come to this?

I focused on controlling my breath, and my emotion, as I heard Rory pick up the bags that had held the money.

I didn't know where he was going to hide, but I tried not to think about that.

Instead, I thought of my dad, again. I thought of that last visit with Dr Richards, again.

I thought, "Louis Armstrong, you absolute fool."

CHAPTER 9

I was in that safe for 10 minutes. I don't suffer from claustrophobia, but due to the size of the safe and how limited my space was my mind began to show frailty after I had been in the safe for 3 minutes.

"What if you never get out of here? He's probably left you; this was the plan all along. What if as soon as someone opens the door you get shot straight in the face?"

My thoughts were interrupted by the sound of footsteps. They were close now, closer than they'd ever been. I couldn't tell if they were inside or outside the office.

"I'll go check the front door, you make sure they're not in this area," a female voice called out.

There was no response, but I heard one set of footsteps and then another shortly after.

I heard a loud bang, followed by what sounded like a quick shuffle.

A few moments of silence before the same sequence occurred.

After the third time I heard footsteps coming towards the office.

"Nothing in the female toilets, over," a male voice spoke this time, a hiss of static followed

"Keep looking, she is here, over."

"Copy that, Captain."

What the fuck? Were these guys cops? Why were cops here?

More importantly, why did the, "Captain" say, 'she'? Like she knew who I was?

The Cost of Good Intentions

Questions kept swirling around in my mind, each fighting for a position at the forefront of my thoughts.

The door burst open with a loud bang, and I heard clearly as the man rushed into the room. This was followed by a lot of heavy breathing. There was grunting, and groaning, and the sound of something clattering to the floor. I was terrified. The struggle lasted for a couple of minutes, but those minutes felt like eternity. I was sure that if Rory did not win that fight they would find me, and I would find out exactly who those people were and why they wanted me. I wasn't sure I wanted to find out.

As quickly as it had begun, it ended. The sounds were rhythmic as both Rory and the man tried to get the upper hand. It was so overwhelmingly intense until the moment all noise ceased, replaced by a singular breath that clawed for all oxygen in its immediate vicinity. I heard a thud as one of the men fell to the floor.

My heart raced as I waited to hear the victor's next move.

Would it be the terrifying beep of a walkie-talkie?

Or the blissful beep of the keypad to the safe?

A few moments passed.

I heard as someone began opening the safe. The dim light blinded me as the door opened, before it was covered by the edges of Rory's dark hair.

His eyes were chaotic, his mouth had blood in the corner. His hands shook as his white knuckles grasped the handle of a knife that was so red you could not see the silver metal anymore.

I hurried out of the safe and hugged Rory. Tears streamed down my face as I looked over his shoulder and saw the bloody body of a man in police uniform. His eyes wide open, his body lying in a pool of blood that was expanding. His radio on the floor next to him, an arm's length away.

Rory didn't hug back.

I knew that he had just lost a piece of himself.

We were interrupted by the sound of the radio.

"Edwards, what's your status? Over."

We didn't respond

After a few moments she asked again.

Rory wasn't moving, he was still holding the knife, looking blankly ahead. I knew I had to do something.

I rushed to officer Edwards body and started searching his pockets. I found a wallet, some house keys and keys to a Ford. My eyes couldn't help but notice the thick gold ring on his left hand.

The female officer asked the same question, sounding more desperate with each word. She sounded like she was running. We had to be fast.

I grabbed Rory and began pulling him towards the door. He didn't offer much help. We exited the office and rushed through the corridor; my arms were burning as I pulled Rory towards the emergency exit. Money was flying out of his pockets, leaving a direct trail to us. I couldn't stop to clear our trail, we just had to get out of that store.

I pushed the bar on the door down and opened the door, rushing outside into a dark car park. There was a fence surrounding the carpark, and on the other side was a lot of trees that we could escape into. The fence was a bit high, but there wasn't anything to stop us climbing it. I pulled Rory to the fence and stopped.

The Cost of Good Intentions

We were stuck, unless he was willing to climb.

He still held on to the knife in his hand, still with a vacant look in his eyes. I couldn't leave him; he had done this for me. He had shattered himself for me.

"Rory, we need to climb, or she will catch us."

He didn't even flinch.

"Rory, I am sorry about what happened, but we need to climb, or she will catch us."

Still nothing.

"Rory, if she catches us, she will hurt me."

A flicker.

He dropped the knife and began climbing the fence.

I began climbing the fence shortly after.

We made it over, both of us jumping from the top of the fence to the hard floor on the other side.

As our feet loudly connected with the ground, I heard the door behind us burst open.

The female officer sprinted outside with one hand on her holstered gun. Rory was quicker off the draw; he was already beside me with his pistol aiming straight for the female officer.

She noticed this and raised her hands. I watched as a grimace formed on her face.

"This is for Edwards," she was so quick in drawing her gun that I didn't even have time to turn before she fired two shots at us.

The first hit the tree beside Rory's foot with the second planting itself in the dirt between his legs.

We both turned and ran into the forest as we heard a few more bullets hit trees and sand.

The Cost of Good Intentions

The shots continued, even as it became clear that we were safe. The trees and darkness both playing their part in concealing our escape. We carried on running until the only sound that we could hear was that of our footsteps and laboured breath.

We were deep in the forest when Rory slowed down, and eventually stopped. His hands rested on his knees; a thin layer of sweat had formed on his forehead with some droplets falling carelessly to the ground. The blood on his face had dried and the rivulets of sweat had helped clear some of it away. His wounds were bad, but not as bad as they seemed with the initial blood covering his face.

I stopped beside him, putting my hands on my knees as well.

The edges of my blonde hair blocked my peripheral vision as I desperately tried to catch my breath. My lungs burned; my legs ached. I couldn't stop myself from vomiting into the soil beneath my feet.

My mind was racing. I had too many questions, and not enough answers.

He still had some of the money in his pockets, and when I saw it, my anger returned. We wouldn't have been in this mess if he hadn't tried to steal the money in the first place.

"I was beside the door, He rushed in and had his back towards me, I got him in a chokehold. I just wanted to knock him out, Amy, but he was so strong. He was too strong. He broke free and elbowed me in my face; he looked me in the eye as he pulled out the knife. I didn't know what else to do, I threw a stapler at him, and while he focused on that I managed to get my hands around his hand with the knife, and then..." Rory cried, saliva bridging together his top and bottom lips.

"I didn't want to do it Amy, I swear, I just wanted us to be safe. The way he looked at me, it was the kind of look someone gives you when you've taken everything they have. He hated me, Amy, and he didn't even know me," his sobs intensified until he couldn't bear to stand anymore. He sat on the muddy floor and held his legs close to his chest.

"It was him or us, Amy. It was him or us."

They teach you everything in school, from calculus to painting. They don't teach you what to do when your best friend is falling apart, there's no blueprint for that. What do you do when the lines of morality have blurred so much that you can't even figure out what's wrong or right anymore?

I didn't know whether to hug him for saving my life or to slap him for putting me in danger in the first place, and for what? A piece of paper that doesn't hold any value. It must be instinctive, almost primitive at this point, that even in a world of chaos the first priority, before safety, is that piece of paper. Officer Edward's wife lost her husband that day, and I lost some part of my best friend. I watched as Rory, a newly broken man, cried like a toddler as he struggled to adjust to the extra weight he had to carry. I decided to hug him. Not because I forgave him, but because I understood that whatever I was thinking, he had probably already thought ten times over. Nobody is a bigger critic of a person than themselves.

The Cost of Good Intentions

His sobs had slowed, his chest returned to a normal rhythm. The last of his tears had dried up as we sat, side-by-side, looking out at the towering trees before us. The dark sky had no stars in it, the moon a distant memory as my mind began to try and make sense of the sun's disappearance.

I had a thought just then. How was I able to see Rory?

The darkness of a true night often engulfed areas like this. There was no light around us, and yet, I could see the little stones on the ground, as if it were the time just after sunset. When it's dark, but not the same as the dark present at midnight.

"What now?" I asked.

"Well, we left the supplies behind, and I don't think we can go back for the time being. Where else can we get food?"

"I'm not sure. I don't really know where we are right now. Probably best to keep walking until we get out of the forest."

"Probably," he stood up, holding out his hand to help me up.

I took it, brushed myself off and we started walking again. I heard his stomach grumble.

"Here," I reached into my pocket, feeling around for a bar of chocolate I had slipped into my pocket in the store. Officer Edward's wallet fell out of my pocket when I pulled the chocolate out. Rory took the chocolate, and I leaned down to pick up the wallet.

"Thanks. What's that?" he asked as he burst the wrapper open and took a bite of the chocolate as we started walking again.

"It's that cops wallet, I thought maybe we could try find out more about him to help figure out what's going on."

"That's good thinking."

"I also got his car keys in case we needed to get out of here," I looked at my feet, I could tell Rory had started looking at me.

"What do you mean?"

"You know, like, out of this city. Somewhere new."

Something shifted in him, I could tell he was thinking about it. We had talked about it in the past, but life in Nod seemed to always have a way of pulling you back into its gluttonous claws.

"Is there a license in there?" he asked calmly.

I opened the wallet and the serious face of officer Kyle Edwards stared back at me.

"Yeah, why?"

"We need to go to his house; his address should be on there. I need to talk to his wife, tell her what happened."

"I don't think that's the best idea, Rory. Intentional or not, you killed her husband."

"She needs to know I'm not a monster, Amy. She just has to."

I didn't like the idea, but Rory seemed like he needed this, so I reluctantly agreed.

CHAPTER 10

We made it out of the forest and managed to establish that we were about 2 miles from officer Edward's house on St. Vincent Street. The street itself wasn't too far from the Super-market, so we made sure to be on our guard as we got closer. St. Vincent street was like any other, houses looked like they were copy-paste versions of their neighbours. Each one adding to the feeling of mundanity that was ever present in Nod. Cars lined the sidewalks as this particular middle-class area was of the poorer variety and didn't include garages to house the mediocre assortment of vehicles that could naturally be found in areas of higher status. We approached number 66; a blue Ford Focus was parked on the pavement next to an average sized grey house. I pulled the keys out of my pocket and tried to open the car. The orange lights flashed when I pressed the unlock button and a sound indicated that the doors had been unlocked. It confirmed that we were in the right place.

The lights of the house were off; all the lights of every house on the street were off. There was no movement, whatsoever.

"We have to wait," Rory insisted, almost reading my mind questioning what to do next.

"Okay, but not outside. I don't think it's safe."

"Agreed, I'll go try the door to see if it's unlocked."

"No need. Catch," I took the house keys out of my pocket, and threw them to Rory

The Cost of Good Intentions

He caught them and looked to see if he could identify which one was likely to be for the front door.

There were no markings, or indications, so I patiently waited as he tried each of the keys before he was able to turn one and open the door.

The house was dark. A lot darker than outside. We slowly walked through the entrance corridor. The first door on our right led to a spacious lounge with laminate flooring. An L- shaped couch was in the farthest corner of the room. There was a wooden table in the centre with a bunch of lilies next to a picture of two children. The grey curtains were drawn, but the room was definitely the brightest in the house as the window received light from the streetlamp directly outside. As we continued further into the house, we spent less time taking in the details as everything reminded us that we had taken away someone's husband, someone's father.

Whether I wanted to admit it or not, I was equally responsible for everything that had happened. A feeling overcame me, an uneasy feeling that gnawed at my insides as I struggled to neglect the truth.

Rory may have stabbed officer Edwards. Kyle Edwards.

But I was not innocent. All the times he had stolen from those drunk men I accepted it as a necessary evil. Comforting myself with the thought that I was not the one doing the crime, but subconsciously understanding that I was benefiting from it.

Maybe if I had been more forceful in my rejection of his crime, of our crime; maybe Kyle Edwards would still be alive, and we wouldn't be averting our eyes from the pictures of a newly formed widow, and two fatherless children.

My thoughts were abruptly halted when we reached the bedroom, which was at the end of the corridor. The wooden door creaked as Rory pushed it open to reveal the gruesome, bloody, lifeless bodies of Kyle Edward's wife and kids.

I ran to the toilet and desperately held the sides as I vomited for the second time that day.

Rory had the same blank expression on his face as he had a few hours before. I wasn't sure if I would be able to help him that time.

"What the fuck is going on?" I asked, still clutching the toilet bowl.

"I'm not sure," his voice was blank, his face expressionless. He was in shock.

"Rory, I'm scared"

"Me too, Amy," he still didn't look away from the bodies.

I got up, my legs shaking underneath me. I needed to be strong, for both of us.

"Come," I gently took his arm and ushered him toward the lounge. I helped him sit on the couch, before placing the picture of the children face-down on the wooden table.

"At least none of them have to live without the other," I said in a feeble attempt to comfort him as I sat next to him on the couch.

"I suppose," he was still looking straight ahead, like a zombie. "I just want to sleep for a bit. Okay. Yeah, just to sleep for a bit. That'll help," he laid on the couch and closed his eyes, it only took a few minutes for him to fall asleep.

The Cost of Good Intentions

I watched him closely, as I contemplated whether I was ever going to be able to sleep again.

That's the thing about grief, everyone does it differently. Some people constantly relive the trauma, while others ignore it completely.

"Amy," Rory whispered in his sleep. "I'm sorry for trying to take the money."

"It's okay," I whispered. A tear rolled slowly down my left cheek. I sat staring at the wall for hours before I closed my eyes and tried to go to sleep.

I woke up when I felt Rory stand. I wiped my eyes as my vision began to clear. I wasn't sure what time it was; I wasn't even sure if it was 'day' or 'night'.

"Morning. Evening. Whatever," I said after yawning.

"We need to try find out what is going on, but first, let's eat something," Rory jumped straight to the point.

I got up and we walked to the kitchen, both of us not looking anywhere near the bedroom. At least there wasn't a smell yet, but I wasn't sure how long that would be the case.

We entered the kitchen, and I started rummaging through the fridge while Rory looked in the cupboards.

We decided that we were going to have standard peanut butter sandwiches and some coffee. This seemed like the easiest way to satisfy our hunger. I put the kettle on and prepared the coffee as Rory made the sandwiches. We sat down on white plastic chairs and put the plates onto the glass table that was directly below a window looking out into the back garden.

The Cost of Good Intentions

The garden was neat, with an assortment of flowers in a flower bed that surrounded the well-maintained grass. A lone football was in the back of a mini football net. I took a sip of the coffee and then a bite of the sandwich. My stomach groaned in thanks for what would be my first meal since the day before, with all that has happened, food was one of the last things on my mind.

"There is something that isn't right about all of this, Amy. I don't know where the sun is, but I don't think it's an accident that it's missing."

"What do you mean, Rory?" I stopped looking out the window and looked at him as I took another bite of the sandwich.

"I mean exactly that. The timing of everything, it's just...*off.*"

"Well, they've been talking about that global warming stuff for years, maybe this has something to do with that?"

"No, I don't think so. The temperature outside seems pretty normal, which doesn't make sense considering the circumstances, but there's something else that I can't quite put my finger on. Those officers didn't seem to be reacting to the store alarm. We were in Super-Market for ages before they even arrived, I had even stopped the alarm by the time they arrived. How did they know we were still there? More importantly, why did the captain say, "she" on the radio? That isn't something you say unless you're looking for someone specific. Did you do something, Amy? Why were they looking for you?"

"I don't know, honestly, the more I think about it the more I think it was a case of mistaken identity."

The Cost of Good Intentions

"I don't think so. The captain saw both of us. I was further away, why did she not even take one shot at you?"

I felt my temperature rise, I wasn't hungry anymore. I put my half-eaten sandwich back onto the plate.

"So, you think I'm some wanted criminal? I'm glad that when all that stolen money was falling out of your pocket, you took the time to notice exactly who she was shooting at."

"So much for it being okay then. Why do you even stay with me? I never hear you complain when money like that gets used to keep you warm and fed in the winter. Does your conscience only let you shit on injustice that doesn't work in your favour?" his voice was loud and firm; an ugly sneer took over his whole face as he stood up, nearly knocking his chair over.

"Fuck you, Rory," I stood as well. "You know what? Maybe it is time we part ways. I've stayed because I care about you, you asshole, but clearly it just takes a little nudge for you to think the worst of me. For years I've gone along with your silly charade, following you everywhere, investing in every plan you've made."

"While in the back of your mind you think of me as a petty thief."

"That's not true, and you know it. I just wanted better, better for the both of us."

"And I never? Tell me, Amy, have you told anyone, but me, about your little project?"

"No." It came out as a whisper. I looked away from his eyes, my shoulders converging as my whole body tried to retract into itself.

The Cost of Good Intentions

"That's what I thought. Your project relies on me, on the money that I have provided over the years. So don't try to stand there and act like you're so much better than me when your use of me doesn't fit within your moral terms and conditions. Don't try to tell me that my necessary evil is so much worse than yours, when I steal from a stranger, and you exploit your dearest friend. Don't you dare stand there for one more second and try pretend that I haven't invested in your plans equally as much as you have in mine."

I couldn't look at him. I knew he was right, about all of it. Rory may have been a thief, but his intention was always pure. He got his hands dirty so mine could stay clean.

"I don't know why they were looking for me, I can't think of anything I might have done that would make them look for me," I said as I stared at my feet.

I glanced up to see a shift in his eyes. He started to calm down and took a moment before responding.

"We need to search the house, see if there are any clues to tell us what happened here."

"I'll look inside," I said, as an unspoken peace offering. I didn't want him anywhere near the room with officer Edward's family.

"Okay, thanks. I guess I'll look outside then for signs of forced entry, or anything else."

"Here," I took the keys to the car out of my pocket and gave them to him. "Check the car and start it."

"Okay," he walked to the front door, and headed outside.

I didn't know where to start, I wasn't sure I wanted to go back into the bedroom, but everything in the house seemed like it was exactly how it was supposed to be, apart from that room.

I was going to have to look, whether I wanted to or not, to try and find answers.

I walked slowly toward the bedroom; the door was still open. Walking towards it, from this angle, I could see a clock on the wall.

21:55

I hadn't ever had a job, and yet I still tried to maintain a routine. I remained in sync with the rest of the world, generally, waking up in the morning and going to bed in the evening. We didn't set alarms, because Rory's schedule was more erratic. He slept when he felt it was necessary and woke when he felt rested. That was why this morning was so strange. It was very rare that Rory woke me up, he understood my patterns and I understood his. These patterns often involved him being more of the proverbial, "night owl", with spontaneity often more of a factor in his life, while I maintained a certain degree of discipline. On a normal day I would just be winding down at this time, often with a book that Rory had, "picked up", on his solitary endeavours. Another pang of guilt as the thought crossed my mind. Before entering the room, I had tried my best to convince myself to detach my emotion from the situation I was about to encounter again, but I don't think anything really prepares you for that, no matter how many times you see it. The bodies still lay there, hollow expressions on their face. A true symbol of the disgusting nature of death; an evident reminder of the horror of which we are all capable. Kyle Edward's wife had mid-length brown hair, pure green eyes and a beauty spot on her left cheek that would normally command your attention, if this particular scene wasn't dominated by the bullet hole on her forehead. His children looked terrified as their lifeless arms hugged their mother's waist; while a similar hole was found on the back of each of their heads. Discolouring their blonde mops of hair with a dark red tint. Rory was definitely right about something. Something was...*off*.

I looked around the room and couldn't see any weapons, or anything that could be used to fight off a potential intruder. Considering the circumstances, I found that odd. Everything in the house was too normal. There wasn't any indication that they had been planning to leave. There weren't any signs of anything suspicious, and yet there were three corpses in front of me. I was trying to piece everything together when I heard gunshots.

I froze, my body unable to move as a million thoughts went through my mind. A sick feeling overcame my stomach and, for the third time that day, I vomited. I rushed to the lounge, peeking through the window. I saw it.

I saw a bald man stab Rory.

There were two others, a man with blonde hair and a woman, bleeding behind a car.

I ran to the kitchen. I recklessly flung drawers open, not taking time to think about anything other than getting what I need to kill the bastard that hurt my best friend. In the third drawer I found a knife of my own.

I rushed toward the door, not considering that I would be outnumbered. It didn't matter though. None of it mattered.

The Cost of Good Intentions

My life had never been normal. My mother died the day I was born. She died giving birth to me. I was 15 when my father died from the cancer, 4 and a half years after his diagnosis. The day that he passed was a Saturday. He took me to a theme park, and we went on all the rides together. He bought me iced cream and candyfloss. A man was selling books at a stand next to the, 'Wheel of terror'. My dad bought me a copy of *Wuthering Heights*, even though I kept on insisting on using the money to get make-up instead. All the girls at my school had started to wear it, and they made fun of me for not doing it as well. I watched these girls paint their faces like canvases, creating an image that they wanted everyone else to see.

When we left the theme park, I didn't know we weren't going home. He drove, the car was silent. There was no music blaring through the speakers, no sound from anything really.

"In this life we must sometimes choose hard paths, Amelia. Circumstances force our hand into action that we don't want to take but is necessary."

"I don't understand."

"I am proud of you, and I know your mom would be proud of you as well. Stay focused, Amelia. Stay true to your path and do whatever you need to do to leave your mark on this world. Fill your head with knowledge, of all kinds, be curious, and never settle for anything less. These other people, they don't have what you have, they don't have your courage, or your intelligence. Don't try to fit into crowds that you are better off staying out of."

"Why are you saying this? What's going on?"

The Cost of Good Intentions

"I am weak. I have arranged with a doctor to put me to sleep. I don't have long left anyway, and this way avoids a lot of pain," he didn't look at me once. "I'm taking you to a place where they'll take good care of you."

I was sobbing as we pulled up outside of an orphanage.

"There is a bag in the boot. They're expecting you."

"I don't want to go, please, don't leave me," I was hysterical.

"Please, don't make this harder for me than it already is. I love you so much my precious girl."

"I love you, too, daddy."

I got out the car and grabbed the bag from the boot. As soon as I shut the boot I watched as my dad drove away. I was quite hurt when he did, but as I got older and my perspective changed, I realized that he couldn't stand to watch me go. It was just as hard for him to leave, as it was for me to be left.

Something good did come out of that day.

As I walked up the stairs of the orphanage, tears streaming down my face. I saw a boy outside of the building. He was dirtier than any boy I'd seen, his clothes were ripped and ragged. His hair looked like it hadn't been washed for weeks.

"You don't want to go in there," he said, matter-of-factly.

"Oh yeah, and why not?"

"Because places like that break your spirit. It's quite sad, to see so many kids get taught fear instead of curiosity."

"Order breeds familiarity, familiarity can be used to help determine and improve upon outcomes, making environments and circumstances better than before due to the advantage of being able to accurately anticipate various possibilities."

"That sounds awfully scripted, in my opinion, but it does make sense now, because through all their order they were able to convince you that they've somehow made my life better, or yours. The girl walking up the stairs of an orphanage, with nothing but a suitcase and an, admittedly, great book."

"The system never stops working, one of these days it will start working in my favour. Out of curiosity, what would a dirty, homeless boy know about books?"

"Plenty, in fact, I've got classics stashed in every corner of this city. I would put good money on it that I know more about literature than three of you combined, and yet you've been 'educated' while I have not."

I liked the boy. Not because he was a non-conformist, but because in all the chaos of that day, all the confusion that had consumed me since exiting that car, he made sense. He lit something inside me that I didn't understand at the time.

"You suppose I'll be better off with you then?" I asked.

"I'd put my house on it."

I turned around and walked down the stairs toward the boy. I stopped in front of him and dropped my bag beside me. The boy stared at me; he was a head taller.

"I'm Rory, by the way."

"Amelia," I replied, timidly.

"Well, Amy, let's get going."

"Where?" I asked.

"Everywhere."

CHAPTER 11

The street was silent when I got outside. I didn't see the three people I had before. I looked both directions of the street, my chest expanding and contracting at a rapid pace. I couldn't hear anything over the sound of my breath. It was overwhelming me as I looked for any indication that they were still there. I heard a cry, and I rushed forward.

On the other side of the car was Rory, in a pool of blood. He was crying; his eyes were manic as he looked at me.

"Amy," he cried, "Amy, help me."

I ran to his side and fell to my knees beside him. I didn't know what to do. There was so much blood, everywhere. I tried to lift his shirt to look at the wound, but it was caught underneath him. When I tried to lift him up, to free the shirt, he cried in pain. The blood wasn't stopping, I watched him get weaker and weaker. Seconds passed, and with each one I could see he was fading. His eyes met mine, an understanding was passed between us in that moment. We both knew he wasn't going to make it. I never got the opportunity to comfort my dad in his dying moments, but I would not let the opportunity to comfort a boy who saved my life, in more ways than one, pass me by.

"Thank you for your sacrifice. Thank you for gifting me your innocence so mine could stay intact. You saved me that day outside the orphanage, and I will never be able to repay you for that. You -"

"Stop," he whispered, "Maybe I did save you outside that orphanage, but you've saved me every day since."

I watched the life leave his eyes. A line of blood trickled down the side of his mouth. His teeth were stained red.

One of Newton's laws states that energy can never be created, or lost, it can only be transferred.

I could feel the energy of this moment, the energy that Rory held, transfer to me. It was instantly converted, from a warm defiance to an unbearable rage. The people who did this had to pay. The bald man had to pay. I wanted him to suffer, to beg me for mercy as I denied him. I wanted to crush everything he ever loved, to the point where he had absolutely nothing left.

I screamed into the air. A deafening screech. I didn't care if anyone heard me. I didn't care who was looking for me. I didn't care where the sun had gone. Everything was unimportant, the only thing that mattered was finding the bald man and making him pay.

I closed Rory's eyes. His face was cold as my fingers brushed over the top of his eyelids. I stood up and turned, leaving his lifeless body behind. I was looking for something, anything, that would lead me to the bald man. I found it. Behind the car; where the woman was, there was blood. The blood continued all the way down the street, heading toward the poorer side of Nod. I had a trail.

I needed to prepare myself. I needed food and a change of clothes. I was walking back to officer Edward's house when, out of the corner of my eye, I saw the pistol on the street. I walked over and picked it up, opening the chamber to check how many bullets it contained. There were only 3 bullets left in the chamber. The rest would be under the bridge where we were sleeping. I couldn't go there now, I needed to follow the bald man before his trail went cold.

I walked into the house, straight into the bedroom, once more. I didn't even care that the bodies were still in there. I opened the cupboard and helped myself to a black hoody, black trousers and a thick black jacket. I went into the children's room next. It was the first time I had been in the room. There were bunk beds in the corner. Posters of various movies lined each of the walls. Toys were scattered on the floor, and in the corner was exactly what I was looking for.

I picked up the schoolbag, opened it and dumped its contents onto the floor, and went to the kitchen to fill the bag with any food that I could find, that wouldn't go off in a few days.

I had everything I needed.

I walked outside and went straight to the car. I could see the keys on the front seat, Rory must have been busy when the bald man and his friends showed up. I was glad I didn't have to search for the keys in the pockets of his lifeless body.

I climbed into the car and threw the backpack onto the back seat.

One of the many disadvantages of being homeless was that at no point did I ever get taught how to drive. I had just seen other people do it, like my dad, or the people stuck in traffic while me and Rory walked beside them. I paid a lot of attention when they were doing it, but you can only learn some things by doing them, and driving is one of those things. You can't ever know how sensitive the pedals are, or when to change gears, without actually being in control of the car. I was learning that the hard way. It took a few attempts for me to discover that you had to push the clutch pedal in as you turned the key for the car to start.

Once I had figured that out, I pushed the clutch in again and put the car into first gear. I tried to gently press the accelerator. The car rocketed forward, bouncing uncontrollably, I felt the force with my entire body as the car was speeding forward, toward the back of a parked Toyota Corolla.

I hit the brakes, not enough to stop the car, but just enough to get some sort of control.

Firmly gripping the steering wheel, I veered clear of the parked Toyota and firmly into the middle of the road.

Beads of sweat dripped from my forehead as I concentrated harder than I ever have in my entire life. My eyes were scanning the street, now that I had control of the car, I needed to find the trail.

I managed to find little spots of blood, illuminated by one of the streetlights on the desolate road.

I followed the trail, only stalling the car twice, from St. Vincent street to the corner of Enoch street.

Just in front of a block of high-rise flats was an empty trolley. I parked the car outside the building, stalling a third time as I forgot to take the car out of gear.

I didn't take the bag from the seat. I only made sure that I had the knife, which I tucked into the waist of my black jeans, and the gun, which I held in my sturdy hands.

Three bullets.

Three people.

One for each of them.

The Cost of Good Intentions

When I reached the trolley, I pushed it aside and looked through the door. The trail carried on up the stairs, it got thicker the higher I got. I noticed a few lights on in the building as I followed the trail all the way up six flights of stairs until I reached a green door. Paint was peeling off the door's corners, the number 13 was terribly faded. I stopped for a moment, composing myself. Thinking of the best way to do this, to get my revenge.

No.

Not my revenge.

Rory's revenge.

I felt dizzy with all the emotion swirling through my body. I couldn't make up my mind.

That's when I heard laughter.

That's what sent me over the edge.

I kicked the door in, and the three of them looked at me. They were surprised, but on top of that, all three of them were either high or drunk. The smell of marijuana filled the air, three empty bottles of vodka laid sideways on the floor.

None of them moved, they all knew they were in trouble, and they weren't in any state to do anything about it.

These three pathetic people had taken everything from me, and they had chosen to laugh, and drink, and smoke, and enjoy themselves after they tore my world apart.

I would have shot them, there and then, but that was a mercy I couldn't afford to give them.

That was too easy, too painless compared to the agony I felt.

"We don't want any trouble, man," the blonde man said, he had a black eye, dried blood all over his face. Even in this time of desperation his voice had an element of calmness, the kind of calmness you would associate with a koala, or a sloth.

"Shut the fuck up!" I shot one bullet through the wall behind them. All three of them flinched at the sound of the gun and instinctively put their hands up. "If I don't ask you to speak, you shut your mouth, unless you want me to shoot you, right between the legs. Do I make myself clear?"

Silence

Another shot, this one out the window.

"I asked if I make myself clear!" I shouted, spit flying in their direction.

"Yes," all three said in unison.

"Good, now blonde boy, get up and get that bitch off the bed."

The woman looked a mixture of shocked, scared and confused.

"I can't, man, she's too heavy for me to lift by myself, besides. I don't think I can even stand right now."

"Did I ask for excuses, or did I ask you to get her off the fucking bed?" I unloaded the last bullet into the wall, right beside his head.

"Alright, alright," I watched him get up, holding the wall for balance, and move toward the woman on the bed. The bald man was still staring at me, his bloodshot hazel eyes laser focused, his hands unwavering as they remained raised above his shoulders in some showing of surrender.

"I want to know what this is about," his voice was deep and calm.

"What do you not get about only speaking when you are spoken to?" I said as the blonde man tried to get his body underneath the woman's arm to support her.

"Then shoot me, because I know that you being here has nothing to do with survival. It has nothing to do with figuring out what's going on either, or you would have stopped somewhere else. So, forgive me for not wanting to follow your rules without knowing why you're setting them in the first place."

"Did you let Rory answer you before attacking him, and stabbing him on the street?" my voice was hoarse. My body was betraying me, sadness flowed through every cell of my body at the cost of saying his name, out loud.

"Well, maybe he shouldn't have shot at us first."

"Bullshit!" Rory wouldn't do that, "Rory never shoots without reason!"

"Is that what all of you homeless trash tell each other?"

"Cole!" the woman had found her voice.

"Don't worry Beck, she would have shot me if she had any more bullets."

I dropped the gun, he rushed to his feet. My hand instinctively reached for the knife. Cole knew what I had. He knew I planned to fill him with tiny little punctures and watch as he bleeds out on the shitty brown carpet. The blonde man, and the woman, Beck, didn't move as they watched the space between me and Cole close in an instant.

The knifes blade glistened, itching for flesh.

A bullet fizzed passed my head and made a clean hole through the blonde man's left eye socket.

Beck screamed as she fell back onto the bed.

I raised my hands, the knife still firmly in my grip as I stopped running towards Cole, and looked at him straight in the eye, a few feet apart. I knew who shot the blonde man, I just didn't want to believe what I knew to be true.

I entered this building thinking I was the predator, forgetting that I was still prey.

"It almost feels like Christmas, Cole Clay, Amelia Clark, and Rebecca Kelser all in the same room. I am getting a bonus for sure," the captain couldn't keep the delight out of her voice.

"What do you want?" I asked, my back still turned. Cole looked confused, as did Rebecca.

"I want a nice big house, a shit ton of money, and all of you to get into the back of my car."

"Why would we do that?" Cole asked, regaining some composure, he was getting more sober by the minute, I could see it. His face was clearing up, his speech less slurred, his eyes more alert as the wheels in his head visibly turned.

"Because there's some very nice people who want to see you."

Cole was so quick. The inches between us closed. I felt him grab me, with surprising force. In one quick motion he had spun me around, my hand that still held the knife was now pointing toward me, the sharp blade brushing against my throat.

I was looking at the captain, she gripped her gun firmly. She wasn't smiling. She was furious.

"Consider your next move, very carefully, Mr. Clay."

"Or what? You'll kill us, like Brad? I don't believe you. If you wanted to kill us, we would already be dead. Now you listen to me, because I am so tired of having people like you determine how I live my life. You're going to answer my questions now, or I am going to slit her throat. Who's looking for us? Why do they want us? And where is the fucking sun?" Cole yelled.

A moment passed; the captain looked like she was contemplating it. She opened her mouth to speak when there was a loud bang and her body fell to the floor. A short man was standing behind her, a pistol in his hand.

"Malcolm?" Cole and Rebecca said in unison.

"Mole, Beck. Where's that piece of shit, Elon?"

CHAPTER 12

COLE

I still had the knife to the woman's throat when Malcolm walked into my shitty apartment. He was careful to step over the body of the female officer he had just shot, calmly placing the pistol in a holster on the side of his trousers. Out of everyone in the room Malcolm looked the calmest. With everything that was going on it was difficult to guess exactly how it was possible for him to take the time to remember to insult me. Looking at him now, you could argue that this was just a typical day for him.

"I don't think I stuttered, Mole. Where is Elon? You always were slow, but this is a new level."

"What are you doing here? How did you know where I live?"

"*What are you doing here? How did you know where I live?*" Malcolm said, in a condescending tone, "You work for me, I have all your personal records."

"Worked. Past tense," I said angrily, "and that doesn't give you the right to use that information whenever you want, Malcolm."

"Actually, Mole, I don't know if you've noticed but these are not exactly, normal times."

He was right about that. For one, in normal times he wouldn't set foot near that side of town, let alone my apartment. In normal times he would have called the police, not shot them, if I had a knife to someone's throat.

"Who's your friend?" He asked, smiling at Amelia.

"None of your business, you fat hobbit," Amelia retorted. Beck let out a snicker. I had to stop myself from doing the same.

I got angry at the thought. She was not allowed to make me laugh. She stormed in there, accusing us of all sorts of things. Threatening us. If Rory had shot a bit higher Beck would be dead. If she didn't come to my apartment, then Brad might still be alive. I held the knife closer to her throat, pressing it into the skin beneath her chin. Malcolm watched me, studying the clear rage behind my eye. He was sick, it looked like he was enjoying what was happening. So, I calmed myself. I would not give him satisfaction, in any way, shape, or form.

"Better tie that one up before she bites your hand off, Mole," Malcolm took the handcuffs from the dead police officer. He walked over, took Amelia's hand and cuffed her to the radiator pipe right next to us. He left his hand on hers too long, giving her time to grab it and bite as hard as she could. He howled in pain and yanked his hand free. I put the knife into the waistband of my trousers.

"Do you know where Elon is, or not?" Malcolm asked while he rubbed his hand, getting clearly agitated by the situation.

"What do you want from him?"

"That bastard told me his people would come fetch me when all this happened," he gestured to the environment. "He took my money and everything."

"What are you talking about?" Beck asked.

"Listen sweetheart, I can't put it in clearer English."

The Cost of Good Intentions

"You're telling me that Elon knew all of this chaos would happen today?" I asked, dumbfounded.

"Knew it? He basically made the whole thing up," Malcolm said and he handed me a card.

When the sun sets, we will rise.

Elon's number was on the back of the card.

"This doesn't mean anything," I said when I finished looking at the card.

Although I couldn't help but admit that it looked incriminating considering everything.

"Maybe it doesn't, but the message he sent me does," Malcolm felt around his body, checking all his pockets for something. "I left my phone in the office."

"How convenient," Beck chimed in.

"What did it say?" Amelia asked.

"I'm not telling *you* anything," Malcolm said with a snarl.

"Considering the fact that we all seem to be looking for answers and you, shit-for-brains, have information that could be useful, maybe you should share it with the rest of us."

I hated to admit it, but she was right.

"I'll ask again, Mole? Who is this filthy woman?"

"I'd rather be filthy than inbred."

"Would both of you stop?!" Beck yelled, she faced me as Amelia and Malcolm gave each other the dirtiest looks each of them could muster. "Cole, it can't be true. We've both known Elon for so long. He would never agree to anything like this."

My eyes wandered to Brad's body lying on the floor. Maybe I was still a bit drunk, or stoned, or both, but none of it felt real when I had the time to consider it. It was crazy, the kind of crazy that shouldn't be real, and yet I knew just how real it was. I knew that all these things were happening and would keep happening. It was the new normal, apparently. So, when I thought of all that had happened, it wasn't so hard to consider the possibility that a man who had lied to my face about Beck, who had a stitched-up bullet wound, could be capable of something like that. I didn't want to be the one to tell her that I believed Malcolm. The lie was too elaborate to make up for such a stupid man. I was about to say as much, but Malcolm, who's pride was hurt from his integrity being called into question, was the first to speak.

"We can go get the phone since you think I'm such a liar, little miss perfect."

He really did have the emotional control of a toddler; it made me wonder how he ever managed to wind me up in the first place.

The familiar sound of the default ringtone on my cheap phone filled the air. I was never a fan of mobile technology, mainly because I didn't ever find it useful. I didn't have anyone to call, and nobody ever called me. It was quite ironic that my phone would be the first to ring. I put my hand in my left pocket and pulled the phone out. It was still in good condition, all things considered. The screen was illuminated as the phone vibrated heavily. The word Elon was written in big letters across the screen.

My heart raced. Everyone was looking at me expecting some kind of explanation, I suppose.

"Well, who is it, Mole?"

"It's Elon," I said, my throat was suddenly extremely dry.

"Pick up, Cole!" Beck's voice was filled with hope, she had even forgotten about her wound for the time being. I felt bad for her. This was the first time that she had ever come across as naïve. If I'm honest I didn't panic when Beck woke me up and Elon was missing. I was more suspicious than anything. It's one thing to tell a lie, but he had been lying to me for years, repeatedly. Something in me changed when I found out the truth about his and Beck's 'relationship'. I had known him for years, and I trusted him, but it was suddenly very difficult to figure out the truth when I hadn't been able to identify multiple lies.

I picked up the phone.

"Cole! Oh, thank God! Listen, Cole, I'm in some serious trouble, I need your help. I-" Elon was whispering.

"Alright, slow down! Stay calm. Where are you? What kind of trouble are you in?"

"I'm at the office, Cole. Some people, they're-"

I heard gunshots in the background. Elon was silent. I checked to see that the call was still connected. It was. I put the phone back to my ear and after a few moments he spoke again.

"I'll explain later, just get here please," his voice was shaky, his breath shallow. "Please, Cole," he hung up the phone.

It seemed that all of our options led to the one place I thought I would never have to set foot into again. I still didn't trust Elon, but we didn't have many other options. Elon had information, and Malcolm's phone had evidence.

"We need to go to the office, Elon is in danger."

"What about her?" Beck asked, gesturing to Amelia.

"We could just leave her here," Malcolm suggested.

"What do they want with you, anyway?" I asked Amelia.

The Cost of Good Intentions

"I could ask the same about the two of you," She looked from me to Beck.

"What does who want with who?" Malcolm asked, clearly confused.

She had a point. Whoever sent the woman officer wanted all of us, and she wanted us alive. I didn't have time to consider why someone would want me, or Beck. My parents no longer spoke to me, and it doesn't seem like it was Elon. I didn't know anything about Amelia either. I couldn't let whoever was looking for us get her, especially since she was clearly important to them.

"Is someone going to answer me?" Malcolm asked.

"No," I said as I walked towards the dead female officer. She had a lanyard with keys on it. I picked it up, as well as the gun from the officer's hand, and walked towards Amelia.

I threw the keys to her and pointed the gun.

"What are you doing, Cole?" Beck asked, concerned "You aren't a killer."

"I'd beg to differ," Amelia said with a snarl, "He seems quite capable of killing."

"Shut up, take the cuff off the radiator and cuff your hands behind your back. When you're done with that drop the keys, if you try anything I will shoot you."

Malcolm licked his lips. His eyes opened a little bit wider, like he was hoping she would try something, just to see what would happen.

She didn't though, she did exactly as I said. I picked up the keys from the ground, now that she was less of a threat.

"We need to take her with," I said to Beck.

The Cost of Good Intentions

"Do I get a say in this?" Malcolm scoffed, clearly still thinking he had any kind of control.

"No, we don't even need you. You're more of a liability at this point."

"Actually, Mole, you're wrong again, as usual. You can't get into the building without my access code at this time of the night."

"Then how did Elon get in?" Beck asked.

"I gave him my code, for out prior arrangement."

"This isn't important, we can just break the door down."

"And just how do you plan on getting to the top floor?"

"We'll take the stairs."

"You mean the stairs that are accessed through the thick steel door? Those stairs, mmmmhm, Mole? You aren't the first to try break into Malcolm Myer's Limited, and let's just say that the other guys were a bit more qualified than you when it comes to burglary, and they still failed. So let me ask you again, do I get a say in this?"

"We can't leave her here, Malcolm. She's valuable, for some reason, we don't know why."

"And you, as well, you're valuable?"

"They want all of us."

"You're valuable, she's valuable, even Beck's valuable, but I am not? That makes no sense, Mole. Who decided that?"

"Welcome to the world, asshole," Amelia chimed in.

"The adults are talking here, sweetheart, we would appreciate it if you didn't disturb us," Malcolm said in his usual condescending tone.

"Don't talk to her like that," Beck said.

"We need to vote then," I said, reluctantly.

"Oh great, at least at the end of the world there's still a democracy. Maybe I should just leave the room while all of you decide my fate," Amelia looked at me, "As much as I hate you, there is no honour in survival, and I'm quite sure that if you leave me handcuffed here, I will be in danger. Whoever is looking for us isn't doing it to have a picnic, and I'm not sure I'd like to find out why they want me, considering it would probably significantly lower my chances of making you pay for murdering my best friend."

"I vote we take her," said Malcolm.

We all looked at him.

"Then why did you intervene when I suggested that in the first place?" I asked.

"Because you said it wrong, Mole. Besides, your ideas are normally stupid."

He was exhausting, I was going to tell him as much when I stopped myself. Malcolm intervened because he was Malcolm, he always had to have a say in everything. Even if I had found out the solution to fixing all of this, he would deny it, not because it wouldn't work, but because he hadn't been the one to come up with the plan.

"Beck, how is the leg feeling?"

"What do you mean how is it feeling, Cole, I was shot a few hours ago, it's fucking sore."

"Okay! I was just asking. It's not like I've been shot before."

"Sorry, I'm just panicking, all of this is overwhelming. I just want to help Elon."

"If you use me as support, do you think you can make it down the stairs and back into the trolley?"

"I think the stairs will be fine, but the trolley seems a little high, I don't think I can manage that sort of pain on my own."

Amelia sighed.

"I've got a car parked outside we can use that to get to your offices. The keys are in my front pocket."

"Let's not waste any more time then," I got the keys from Amelia's pocket and then walked to Beck to help her up. She grunted as she struggled to her feet. One of her legs hovered over the ground. Her arm was around my shoulder. I felt all the weight of her as she leaned on me for support.

"You first," I pointed the gun at Amelia.

She walked out the door. Stepping over the dead officer's body. Malcolm was next, followed by me and Beck. More lights were off as we walked down the steps slowly, mainly because of Beck, but also because we were now on alert. We would have to be like this all the time, I thought. How exhausting. Walking down the stairs I contemplated if all we were doing was even worth it. Did I even want to know what was going on? In 27 years, I probably asked that question the most, and to be honest, I'm not sure I did want to know. Because every time I found out why things were the way they were I was disappointed. Disappointed to discover that, as usual, the culprits of chaos often seem to be delicately intertwined with greed. It would have been quite easy to stop walking to the car, directly to danger, and just go back up to my flat. I could have just laid down next to the two dead bodies, had another drink and joined my soon to be companions in eternal slumber. The constant emotional ache I suffered would be gone, no more sorrow, no more pain, just emptiness.

"Thanks for not leaving me behind, Cole," Beck suddenly said, "You know you could have. I probably would have even understood."

"It wasn't ever an option."

"Why not?"

"Same reason why we need to get to the office to help Elon."

"And what reason would that be?"

"Friends don't leave each other behind," I said as we reached street level.

A blue Ford Focus was parked directly outside the door. I watched as Malcolm opened the back door for Amelia.

"No, she gets in the boot," I said, pointing the gun at Amelia.

"Oh, come on, I'm already handcuffed, it's not like I can escape."

"Actually, I'm not sure what you're capable of. So, I'm not taking any chances. In the boot, now!"

Malcolm opened the boot and Amelia got into it.

I helped Beck into the back seat. Here was the dilemma. Here was why we really needed Malcolm. I was going to tell him he wasn't welcome until Amelia told us she had a car. We could get into the offices just fine, I knew the code, I had seen him use it on several occasions when I stayed late at the office. But right now Beck had been shot and I was too drunk.

"You need to drive," I said, dangling the keys in front of him. A wry smile formed across his face. It looked ugly on him, his features didn't fill the entirety of his too round face, but that smile had something about it. Something sinister. Malcolm Myers was a wicked man, power hungry and desperate for control. When he got it, it was like giving him the best gift he would ever receive, because he needed validation. If you dug deeper into the life of Malcolm, you would come to find that those football pictures in his office were all from one game. The trophies? He got to hold them because he was a reserve on the squad. He didn't see himself as a critical figure in what seemed to be a hugely important time in his life. I don't think he got over that, not really, and that's a horrible shame. If he ever really thought about it, he was instrumental in the success of that team. He was pushing one of the squad members to be better, to stay in the team, and that helped them win those trophies. Yet there he stood, smiling at me with that despicable smile that said, "That's right, I own you, I'm better than you, you would be nothing without me."

The same man who, no doubt, felt inferior, gets satisfaction from making others feel the same. All because, when it came down to it, his perspective was so self-centred that he would never truly be able to see the good he could do in another's life if he just put down the sword that others had used to stab him.

I got into the passenger's seat, Malcolm, still beaming from ear-to-ear, got behind the wheel.

We didn't even make it a block before I was blinded by headlights and my world went dark.

CHAPTER 13

I opened my eyes to bright light. My head hurt as my vision was coming into focus. I was squinting, looking directly into a square LED fitting. I put my hand in front of my eyes, blocking out the blinding light. I tried to sit up, my body resisting. Aching all over. I managed to sit up, I was on a single bed, a table next to me with a glass of water. It was really hot in the room so I grasped the glass and brought it towards me, sniffing its contents before confirming that it was indeed water. I was disappointed. I gulped down the water, my mouth feeling as dry as a desert. I wanted more, needed more. I took my feet off of the bed and had a look around the room. It was massive, but it had a minimalistic feel to it. All the walls were bare and everything in the room was pure white. Including my clothing. There was a bathtub beside a toilet and sink with a mirror in the far side of the room. I looked down at my body and it was hard not to notice how clean I was considering all the blood I had on me before.

Where was I?

What happened?

Where were Beck, and Malcolm, and Amelia?

What was this place?

I tried to stand, but before I made it very far a woman walked into the room. She was a small woman, with short hair. Her golden-brown skin the perfect contrast of her pure white uniform. When she saw me trying to stand, she rushed over, hurriedly putting a tray with food and more water on the table next to me.

"Please, Mr. Clay, sit down. You'll be too weak to stand for the time being."

"Where am I? Who are you?" I asked the nurse.

"You're safe, Mr. Clay. I am your designated servant. Someone would like to see you when you've had something to eat and drink. When you finish these pancakes, and you've had your water just ring this bell and I will come get you with a wheelchair."

I looked at the plate. Fruit loop pancakes. There are only two people in this world who would know that was my favourite breakfast, and one of them had dementia. I couldn't believe it. I was hungry, even just looking at the plate, but suddenly my need to eat seemed less important.

"Please take me to her," I said, trying to stand again.

"Please, Mr. Clay, I must insis-"

"I said, take me to her, now!" I snapped.

"Right away!" she hurried out the room to go fetch the wheelchair. I started scoffing down the pancakes in her absence and gulped down the glass of water. My mouth was full of the last of the pancakes when the nurse returned with the wheelchair.

I tried to swallow what was left in one big gulp. It pained my throat and chest as it made its way down my oesophagus.

The servant helped me into the wheelchair and started pushing me toward the door. We exited into a white corridor. There were doors all along the corridor, left and right, with little windows on them. Each door had a name on it, none of them opened as I was pushed towards a set of double doors at the end of the corridor.

I was amazed when we entered through the double doors.

The Cost of Good Intentions

There were people, everywhere.

Everyone was in swimwear, either relaxing on one of the many available red and white lounge chairs, or swimming in the massive clear blue pool. The noise was deafening as laughter and chatter filled the air while all kinds of drinks were being transported by men and woman in a more exotic variation of the white uniform worn by the woman who pushed my wheelchair. The sun shone in the sky and heat filled the room to provide the final touches of the golden image that I had the privilege of witnessing. Such a scene would cause the most pessimistic being in existence to reconsider their stances. It was pure ecstasy on full display.

My mind had drifted from all my previous thoughts, leaving me void of all suspicion I had held mere moments ago. Instead, I was filled with curiosity, and in turn longing. These emotions often went hand in hand, it was the curse we bore. In this, my moment of ultimate joy, sadness was still present. The sadness that I would, most likely, never experience a moment of this magnitude again. I had experienced this before; it was why I started drinking in the first place. I couldn't bear to understand that I had hit the peak. Reminiscing often bred depression, the kind of depression that only seemed to go away when I emptied the contents of a bottle. That glorious substance took away my longing for a moment like this, giving me a few hours of reprieve before the emotion came back 10-fold.

My hands shook as the nurse forced me to leave my personal Eden and we entered another, less crowded, room where a woman stood. She looked out of the window at a field so green it looked like it had been the reason why the colour was named in the first place. The room had a solitary stone bench in the centre with a monument, inscribed with words I couldn't make out. Behind the bench was a light that shone out of the opposite corner of the room, directly onto the monument.

The servant had placed me behind the woman, a few feet away. The woman had short grey hair, a little longer than a buzz cut. She wore a navy-blue suit jacket matched with the same colour pencil skirt. Her posture was impeccable, as it had always been.

"Thank you, Blessing, you may leave us now," the woman said. Blessing responded with a silent curtsey and left the room. The tip-tap of her white shoes echoing as she did so.

"It's good to see you, Cole, although I must say that you look like shit."

"I see you're as charming as always, mother."

The woman turned around, her hazel eyes looking into mine. The wrinkles on her face were now clearly defined, edging around the corners of her dark red mouth.

"I have to say, I was confused for the entire day, and still am to an extent, but the least surprising thing about today is that you somehow have to be involved in it."

"Flattery will get you nowhere, you know that, son."

"I do, so let's skip the part where you pretend you give a shit about me, and you can do me the curtesy of answering a few questions."

"Contrary to your personal popular belief, I am not the monster you think I am, so I'm sorry if I am going to disappoint you by telling you that you are safe because of me, and I'm just going to need you to trust that."

The Cost of Good Intentions

"Trust? That's a heavy demand coming from you, I wouldn't trust you as far as I could spit."

"That's the second time in less than a minute that you've insulted me, this hardly seems like a solid foundation on which to build our new relationship."

"I don't want anything to do with you, as soon as I can walk, I am getting out of here."

"I'm afraid I can't let you do that. You would only end up compromising what we are trying to do here."

"So, I'm your prisoner then?"

"I don't see any chains, do you?"

"No, but this does feel like I'm in one hell of a cage."

"Always so quick to judge, and slow to listen. If anything, I thought you would at least take the meticulousness from your father. He never scampered over the details before opening his mouth. Too bad all you got was his alcoholism."

I tried to get up again but fell back into the wheelchair, almost immediately. My teeth were borne in a display of rage.

"And his temper, too, it seems. If anything, you should be thanking me. Maybe buying me a cup of coffee, asking me how I've been all these years."

"I think we're past that point, if you wanted coffee, you could have called, instead of just leaving me, scared and alone in that shitty apartment."

"You put yourself in that apartment, I told you that you could have come to work with me and your father. There was always space for you, you just never wanted to take it."

"The same work that had you and dad defending criminals? That work?"

"Innocent until proven guilty."

"That's bullshit, and you know it. Both you and I know that those clients of yours were all guilty, of course that didn't hurt your bottom line."

"I've got a huge file, filled with documents saying that you're wrong, in the court of law. All of that is irrelevant, now, anyway."

"What do you mean irrelevant?"

"Everyone in Clayland has a clean slate."

"Clayland? This place?"

"Yes, this place," She turned to stand beside me, both of us now looking out of the window. "Welcome to eutopia Cole."

"Am I supposed to clap, or something? You haven't even told me what I'm doing here, anyway."

"This is your new home. A new Nod. A place of limitless potential, no hunger, no poverty, just life."

"How did I get here?"

"I had someone pick you up, they said you were quite inebriated when they did."

"Pick me up? Last thing I remember is being hit by a car, when me and my friends were driving to my office. Where are my friends anyway?"

"What do you mean you were hit by a car?" she looked genuinely concerned, but I knew better than to believe her fake empathy.

"I mean that a car drove into the car I was in, with my friends. I'll ask again, where are they?"

"Your friends, Malcolm Myers, Rebecca Kelser and Amelia Clark are all residents in Clayland, you will see them in due time, and have plenty of time to enjoy one of our many leisurely activities together. Now, if you'll excuse me, I must go take care of something."

"No, I have too many more questions."

"So many questions, so much time, a blessing afforded to a select few. I had hoped this conversation would have gone slightly differently, but I cannot control all things it seems. I am looking forward to developing our relationship, Cole."

"Can you, for one second, stop talking to me as a lawyer and talk to me as my mom?"

"Unfortunately, my matter has now become urgent. I will answer any questions you have tomorrow, once you've gotten sufficient rest," she began walking away from me. I contemplated following her, but I knew it would be pointless, she wouldn't tell me anything, because she didn't want to.

"Oh, and Cole?" she looked over her shoulder as I looked over mine. "I'm not a lawyer, I'm the new president," she opened the door and Blessing scurried into the room. A terrified look on her face as she took short quick steps to push me back to my room, presumably.

She took me a different way to the way we had come. All the rooms we went through had see-through walls, each one had different things on display. The first had an assortment of sea-creatures. The second had a selection of wildlife. The third and final room had a variety of birds. I suppose this display was for me, the instruction of my mother to give me a tour of her new kingdom. We exited the room to another corridor, much like the one we came from, the only exception being that this one had further corridors running adjacent to the one we were traversing. I took time to take note of the names to see if there was anyone I recognised.

It was a shock to say that I recognised most of them, most of the names belonged to wealthy, famous people from Nod, with a few exceptions. I continued looking but didn't see the name of anyone with whom I was personally acquainted. I was disappointed as the nurse took me through, yet another, set of double doors.

It was in that corridor that I saw her. Amelia was being carried by a muscular man. She was crying immensely, kicking the man in his shins, screaming deafeningly loud. Her blonde hair tied up, exposing her red face, streaked with tears. Her cheeks were dominated by thousands of freckles which only stood out more due to their stark contrast with her emerald-green eyes. She just kicked, and screamed, and cried. Our eyes met and I was hit with a jolt of emotion. I had no idea why she was so terribly upset. All I knew was that I felt sorry for her. The same woman who had tried to kill me not too long ago was in hysterics, and it was impossible to ignore. She didn't say anything, she didn't have to because I've been there. I know a broken person when I see one. More so, a freshly broken person, one who hasn't had time for the wound to scab. Blessing picked up the pace, my eyes followed Amelia until she disappeared around the corner, into one of the other corridors. We went through another set of doors and before I could turn my head around Blessing had stopped pushing me and had gone to open the door to my room. She pushed me into the room, and I climbed back into the bed. A glass of orange juice was on the table beside my bed.

The Cost of Good Intentions

"Do you have something stronger?"

"I'm sorry, Mr. Clay, but your mother has provided strict instruction not to serve you any alcohol."

"Well, you tell he-" I began to shout, Blessing was startled, her head slightly bowed, her hands clasped together in front of her. "I'm sorry, I'll speak to her later, myself."

"Yes, Mr. Clay, is there anything else I can get for you in the meantime?" she hadn't moved, she still looked terrified.

"No, thank you," my voice was soft as I spoke, I looked away from her as she left the room with her short, quick steps.

There was no clock in the room, no way to tell the time. I hadn't been awake for long, but this was unbearable. My hands were shaking uncontrollably. My mouth was dry, so I drank the juice on the table. It tasted a bit strange. My head was pounding. I craved a remedy; I craved my cure. I grew weaker as I lay in the bed. Not even sure how much time I'd spent staring up at the bright light. Counting the tiles on the ceiling until finally I was given a reprieve. My eyelids grew heavy as my mind lay exhausted, fighting what seemed to be an unwinnable war. I drifted off into the blissful tranquillity of sleep.

CHAPTER 14

I woke in a panic, my eyes shot open to discover that it hadn't been a dream, I was really there. I was in Clayland. I didn't need to move to feel how damp the sheets were from my sweat. I felt nauseous. My stomach hurt as well. I looked next to me at the table. The water had been refilled, there were some tablets next to the glass. I didn't know what they were, but I took them anyway. They didn't completely help me, but they definitely took the edge off. Having regained some control of my body I sat up and put my feet on the floor. I wasn't as sore as I was earlier. I wasn't sure how much time had passed, but something told me that I had been asleep for quite some time. My body was more rigid than usual, like it hadn't been stretched in days. My muscles groaned as I pushed myself up off of the bed and tried to stand. I used the wall to help support me as I fought off a wave of dizziness. When it had passed, I stood normally. Apart from my muscles being stiff I felt okay. I knew I couldn't waste time in there anyway, I needed to get out, needed to find the others, needed to find Elon, needed to find out what was going on.

I pushed open the door to my room. Entering the corridor. It was empty as I turned right and headed for the room where I had spoken to my mother.

I found her in the pool area. The initial amazement was still there, but the edges of the image in my mind now held a dullness where there had once been a glow. She was laughing loudly. A pair of sunglasses covered a large majority of her face. She wore a massive straw sunhat as she lazily laid on one of the lounge chairs, looking at a man in the chair next to her.

She sat up, a bit more alert than before she saw me. A wide smile spread across her face. It was strange to see, my mother didn't smile very often. Unlike Malcolm, her smile felt like it had been crafted just for you, like a cold day where you get an invite into a warm house with a cup of coffee waiting with just the right amount of sugar.

"Cole," she said, still wearing the smile, "I would like you to meet my husband, Ben."

The man who was in the chair next to her turned around to look at me. His one cheek was a brighter red than the other, a smile was plastered to his face as well. His hair was black and was greying around the sides. He had a full beard that was patchy in a few places under his neck. His emerald-green eyes looked at me over the top of his Ray-Ban sunglasses. He wore a solid gold watch on his left wrist.

"It's a pleasure to meet you, son, Eleanor has told me a lot about you," he said, extending his hand in my direction.

"Wish I could say the same. It's a surprise *Eleanor* has told you anything about me, considering she doesn't even talk to me, or know me at all," I left my hands at my sides.

"Cole," my mother glared at me.

"Now, now, honey, it's alright," Ben said to my mom. "We all have our own battles, son, and believe me your mom knows plenty about you."

If that was his way of trying to comfort me, it was pathetic.

"Do you mean to say that she's been spying on me?"

Ben was silent.

"Because it sounds like that to me, and I think there are better parenting strategies than that. Like maybe trying to actually be there for your child, and not attempt to force them into a morally bankrupt job."

"Cole, that's enough!" my mother said sternly.

"I'll decide when it's enough, thank you very much. It'll be enough when you answer my fucking questions. Starting with this one, why are we here?"

Ben had gotten tense. I saw him start to get up from his lounge chair. I looked around and noticed that a lot of the people in here were looking at me. Their expressions neutral as they just stared.

My mother grabbed my arm and ushered me into the room we had last spoken in.

She had let the door slam shut behind us.

She turned to me, taking the sunglasses off her face. Her eyes were filled with rage.

"Don't you ever speak to me, in front of people, like that again! Do you know what they will do if they see any sign of weakness? They will try to take my place, Cole!"

"That's what you're worried about? Them taking your place at the top of this fucked up food chain?"

"Do you know how hard I have worked to get to the top of this 'fucked up' food chain? It's taken my entire life. I have sacrificed a lot to be where I am today, and you aren't going to take that away from me because you, poor little Cole, want to burn the olive branch I have extended."

"You haven't told me anything! What am I doing here? Where are my friends? Where even is here? Before I got here the fucking sun was gone, did you know that? Did you have anything to do with that?"

The Cost of Good Intentions

"You are here because I brought you here, and you will see your friends in due time. I told you that."

"That doesn't mean anything! Just answer me!"

"Fine, you want to see your friends so bad, just fine! I will arrange for you to have time to see them this afternoon, as a favour to you."

"A favour? You owe me that. You owe me more than that for all that you've put me through. All my life you've isolated me, making sure I wasn't making friends, pushing me into things I had no interest in doing. So don't stand there and pretend to be this gracious innocent angel that has moved mountains to give me vague answers to my questions."

"This conversation is over, Cole. You will see your friends this afternoon."

"I don't even know when that is!"

"I'll arrange for a watch for you, now if you'll excuse me, I need to go apologize to my husband for your behaviour," she walked back through the door, towards the pool area.

I decided to walk the other way, I remembered the doors the nurse had taken me through. When I got to the first door, I tried to open it. It was locked. I didn't want to go back through the pool area, so I looked around the room for any other doors. There was one in the opposite corner of the room that was so blended into everything that you would miss it unless you were looking for it, I walked to it and the door was unlocked. On the other side was a room that mimicked that of the cafeteria at my old job. The only differences being that everything was white, to follow suit with the rest of Clayland's theme, and there was a white board in the corner of the room. The board had 4 sections, each labelled with a different job. Cooking, Cleaning, Serving, Pleasuring.

There were names under each one written in a blue marker. The names looked like they had been erased and rewritten, multiple times, like some sort of rota.

I saw another door across the room, it led me into a much darker corridor with doors on the right-hand side. There was a slightly pungent smell in the air. A light flickered while the others seemed dimmer than all the other areas I had been taken to. I looked through one of the glass windows on a door and saw five people sleeping on the floor. I watched as Blessing exited one of the rooms. She let out a yawn, her eyes drooping as she brushed off the invisible creases on her uniform. She saw me and her eyes shot up, she rushed over and ushered me out the door. She was using considerable force, but not enough to make me lose balance. We went back through the canteen area and into the Monument room. It was only then that she breathlessly said, "I'm sorry Mr. Clay, but you aren't allowed through there. That area is for the servants."

"Why were five people sleeping on the floor?"

"That's the families, Mr. Clay, they stay with the workers," she whispered this to me.

"Then why do I have a room to myself?"

She looked confused, like I was supposed to know this by now.

"Because you are your mother's son."

"Why is that important?"

"Because your mother is in charge of Clayland, Mr. Clay."

I never understood that. Here we were, in a brand-new place, seemingly cut off from the rest of Nod, as well as the rest of the world, and yet nothing had changed. The same hierarchy was in place, with me as a beneficiary instead of a casualty, and why? Because fate had decided to make me the offspring of a self-absorbed woman? It made me uncomfortable. In the time that I had been there Blessing had helped me. She brought me food, water, probably was the one to change my clothes and make sure I had enough medicine. All the while she slept in a place that made my apartment look like a five-star hotel. I had never been in a position of power, at any point in my life. I was never someone that commanded respect, probably because the kind of power that people hold is often more influenced by fear than admiration, or gratitude. I had an opportunity, and I was beginning to understand it, an opportunity to help make a change. I wanted better for Blessing. I wanted better for all the other servants in Clayland. I had to show them that I did not hold the same values as my mother, so that they would understand that I was a friend, not an enemy.

"Well, I don't like what's going on here, I'm going to speak to my mother about changing the living conditions for you, and the other servants."

"Please Mr. Clay, do-"

"Call me Cole."

"Mr. Cole you don't ha-" she was still terrified I couldn't understand why. Looking at the way her hands were shaking, and her voice threatening to break filled me with a burning rage.

"It's alright, Blessing. I'm going to speak to her and get you out of that shithole," I was already walking away from her, back toward the pool area. I heard Blessing start crying. I wish I had experienced that moment, the moment where someone finally took the time to really stand up for me and really make a difference in my life. I wish I got to feel the euphoria of knowing that my life was finally going to change. I left the Monument room with a spring in my step, I felt like a hero in some weird way, walking confidently towards the villain with a clear purpose, a new aim. My mother was now at a type of bar area beside the pool (hypocrite). She was leaning on the granite bar counter underneath a thatched gazebo, a wide selection of standard alcoholic beverages was on display behind her slender figure. My mother was speaking to Ben again, her smile had returned. She looked relaxed, as if we hadn't just fought a few moments ago. I was starting to feel nauseous again, and my head was hurting. I needed to lie down, but I wanted to talk to her first.

"Why are there multiple servants in one room?"

Her smile faded a little but didn't disappear entirely.

"Why would you think that?"

"Because I just saw it."

"Ah, well, we are in the process of expanding the parameters of Clayland, unfortunately it has to be like that for the time being while we make space to individually house them."

"Well, that's not good enough, is it?" my hands began to shake again.

"We do the best with what we are given, son," Ben said to me, he was more stern than my mother, like this was some kind of good cop-bad cop play.

"I'm not your son, old man."

The Cost of Good Intentions

My mother did her best in maintaining what was left of her initial broad smile. Ben's face remained unchanged, completely neutral.

"We're working on it, Cole," my mother said to me, "It won't be long until everyone has their own living quarters, okay? Now why don't you go get some rest, you're looking a bit worse for wear."

I didn't want to, but she was right, I was feeling worse and worse by the second.

"I will arrange for some more medicine to help with the withdrawals for you and a watch before your time with your friends later, now go get some rest," her full smile had returned. I couldn't bear to look at it anymore. When I turned around, I noticed the glances, everyone was smiling and frolicking about, but they had definitely been watching us. The interaction between us. Taking mental notes of each detail of an interaction between their leaders and one of their leader's offspring.

It was sickening. These people were scanning us, looking for signs of weakness, that they can exploit. That warm smile that my mother wore suddenly didn't hold as much appeal as it had initially, because I realised how fake it was. All of it, one big charade to give the illusion that they were as close to perfection as you can get. I wouldn't play their game, not here. I wouldn't puff out my chest and walk with a larger-than-life swagger. I walked with an open fragility, not concealing my discomfort. My temperature soaring all the way through my body as I gingerly walked towards the door. I knew what my mother was doing, and I couldn't live by those rules. I was human, and I wanted them to see it.

The Cost of Good Intentions

I got back to my room and, as if they had overheard our conversation, fresh tablets sat next to a new glass of water. On the pillow of the perfectly made bed laid a note. I washed the pills down with water, but the effect was not the same. While I felt a bit better, my head was still throbbing as I picked the note up to reveal a gold watch, just like Ben's, that had been underneath the note.

The note read:

To the start of something beautiful, B

The watch had the time and date on it, 10:43am on the 17th of September 2010.

It had been six days since the sun had disappeared.

Six days since we were on our way to fetch Elon, who was in danger.

A terrible feeling sat in my stomach at the thought. I wondered if I would ever see my friend again.

CHAPTER 15

I heard a light knock on the door before a different nurse walked into the room.

"Good afternoon, Mr. Clay," she smiled at me, carrying a plate with toast, along with water, more tablets, and another note.

I frowned as I sat up to help her, by clearing the table of the empty water glass.

"Where is Blessing?" I asked as I took the tablets.

"Blessing has been assigned to another guest I'm afraid. I'll be taking care of you from now on. Would you like me to feed you while you get ready for your leisurely time?"

"That won't be necessary, I'll manage just fine on my own, thank you."

"As usual, just ring the bell if you need anything," she said, a velvety element to her voice, as she left the room.

I read the note that instructed me to be in the Monument room by 14:00pm. I looked at the watch, now firmly on my wrist, it was 13:32.

I ate the toast and drank the water.

With the new knowledge of the length of time I had been in Clayland, it made me uncomfortable knowing that I had probably been in the same clothing for the last four days. I contemplated ringing the bell and asking for a fresh set of clothing, but I saw that on the pure white wall there was a little black line. I walked up to the line and put my hand to it. It was slightly misaligned with the rest of the wall. A small push and the wall opened to reveal a closet full of all different kinds of clothes. Most of the clothing was more tropical than I would normally wear, with a more limited selection of the dull attire I had become accustomed to wearing. There were no long- sleeved shirts and everything was designer, which made sense when observing the obscure nature of a lot of the clothing.

I settled on a plain black t-shirt with a huge white X proudly displayed in the middle, blue jeans with holes cut into them, and black and white sneakers that came all the way up to my ankles.

Once I was dressed, I went to the Monument room.

My mother and Ben were deep in conversation, looking out the window that overlooked the field. Amelia sat on the stone bench, her back faced the monument. Her eyes had red rings around them, like she had been crying for days. She wore a sundress that had sunflowers scattered all over. Her slender hand held up her chin as she stared blankly into the space ahead.

She didn't move, even though she recognised I had entered the room. My mother and Ben had stopped speaking, they turned to me with their fake smiles plastered on their faces.

"I see you've changed," my mother said as she looked me up and down, "A bit too bleak for my liking but stylish nonetheless. Maybe next time consider going for more radiant colours, like Amelia."

As if I wore what I wore because I wondered if she might like it.

"Please, Cole, have a seat," she gestured to the bench that Amelia was sitting on.

"No, I'd rather stand," I said as I crossed my arms across my chest.

The Cost of Good Intentions

"Have it your way," she was talking in a higher tone than usual, "Ben and I have been thinking that maybe it is better for you to spend time, just with Amelia for now."

"Why? Where are Beck, and Malcolm?"

I could have sworn I saw a little twitch in her left eye.

"They prefer their own company at this moment in time. Besides, I think you and Amelia could use the time to build up your relationship, which I understand to be severely fractured."

I felt uneasy, maybe Malcolm wouldn't want to see us. After all, he didn't care about anyone but himself, and I imagine he would quite like being served all day. I bet his bell is going non-stop. Beck on the other hand, she wouldn't want to be alone. My mother wasn't telling me something, but that wasn't really a surprise at that point.

"Why would I want to spend time with someone who tried to kill me literally 6 days ago?"

"Remember, Cole, everything is forgiven here in Clayland. What happened in Nod should not be held against anyone, it would only sour relationships in our new paradise."

"Can we cut the bullshit, just get to your point so I can go back to dealing with my other problems."

"We've arranged for the two of you to be given time alone in our designated art section, which you will be escorted to in the next few moments. I know how much you like to draw, and Ben tells me that Amelia is quite fond of literature, so we felt it might provide an opportunity for you two to bond over a common interest."

Amelia shifted uncomfortably. She looked to be fighting a fresh wave of tears. She still didn't look at anyone in the room, though.

The Cost of Good Intentions

"It actually shows how little you know about me, I stopped drawing years ago, you would know that if you actually took the time to take an interest in me, other than when it suits you. If we are done here, then please excuse me while I go back to my room to deal with the splitting headache that your tablets don't fix."

"I'm afraid I must insist, Cole," there was a certain malice in her voice.

"And yet you're convinced I'm not a prisoner," I scoffed.

Ben cleared his throat, drawing my eyes towards him. He didn't do it to get my attention, he did it to call in the muscular man servant who I saw carrying Amelia a few days before. His arms had marks all over them. His face showed no emotion as he held open the door that led to the different displays.

"Please follow, Elliot. He will escort the two of you to the art section," Ben said sternly.

Amelia immediately got up, almost running to the door. Her long strides covering huge amounts of ground as she raced out of the room.

I followed, looking at my mother and Ben as I walked out the room. They were still smiling when I walked through the door and left them behind.

Elliot walked in front of Amelia, who walked in front of me. I didn't try to catch up to her. To be honest, I wasn't interested in spending any time with her whatsoever. I wasn't sure why my mother and Ben wanted us to spend time together, anyway, considering that they seemed to know our history.

Elliot opened the doors for us, leading us through each of the display rooms before we entered the corridor that followed. We went into one of the adjacent corridors and turned right at the end of that passage. I tried to keep track of where we were going but after a series of fast left and right turns, I realised that I had started to question my memory, and that I had little to no idea where we were. It wasn't easy trying to keep track of things when all you could focus on was trying to stop yourself from feeling sick.

Elliot picked up the pace in one of the corridors and opened a small gap to me and Amelia before he came to a halt outside a solid white door. He opened the door and ushered us into the room. As I approached, I read the words, "Art Centre", in thick black lettering, printed on the door.

My head was turned as I read the words, when I began to look in front of me again, I had to stop quickly, to avoid barging into Amelia, who had come to a complete standstill. I was just about to shout at her before I was absorbed by the scene in front of me.

The room was split completely down the middle. The left was a section dedicated to all the most famous paintings in human history. Starry Night took centre stage, surrounded by the likes of The Mona Lisa, The Last Supper and The Garden of Earthly Delights. The right had towering brown oak bookshelves that reached all the way to the ceiling. Ladders on wheels were held in the corners of each of the seven double sided bookshelves. The middle of the room had a huge table that stretched all the way to the far end of the room. 20 chairs surrounded the table, each neatly tucked in. It was so refreshing to see a more elemental look in a room of a building that was so bland in comparison.

The Cost of Good Intentions

There was a sketchpad with different kinds of paints, and brushes, and pencils sitting in front of one of the seats on the table. In front of the seat next to it was a notebook with a pen on top of it, beside a copy of *A Tale of Two Cities*.

Amelia walked to the latter, picking up the contents and moving them to the farthest point from the sketchbook. It was clear that both of us were on the same page when it came to the subject of creating a bond.

I sat down and opened the sketchbook to a fresh blank page. I stared at it for what felt like an eternity. I didn't even pick up a brush when Elliot announced, in a thick husky voice, that our time was up. I was escorted back to my room, and I couldn't think of anything else, other than that blank page. I looked at my watch to notice that it was already 19:00. I had been trapped in my own head for five hours, not even thinking about my shaking hands, my sore head, and my aching stomach as I was once again reminded of their presence as I regained active consciousness.

I hadn't felt like that in so long. A spark had lit inside me in those five hours, awakening muscles that had been lying dormant for years.

I felt like I had got something back.

The days blurred into weeks, weeks into months, each one was a carbon copy of the one before, yet something had changed. I saw less of my mother and Ben, which was a welcome occurrence. I followed the same routine. Waking up to different variations of my favourite food. Amelia and I were given complete access to the Art Centre between

The Cost of Good Intentions

14:00 and 19:00 every day, in some hope that we would miraculously become best friends. All that mattered was the access, the rest was irrelevant. My withdrawal symptoms became more manageable, it helped that I didn't have any time to think about anything other than that room, and any lingering pain was taken away from the tablets. Every couple of days I entered the room to more paintings, while the bookshelves were noticeably more consumed by new literature. Before long, the room next to the Art Centre became a continuation. A whole extra room dedicated to all the things I was rediscovering. My imagination burst into life. The images flowing through my brain quicker than I could put each delicate line onto paper. Amelia had stopped coming a few weeks after we had entered the centre for the first time. The day after she stopped coming I found a copy of a book called *Animal Farm* on top of my sketchpad. It stayed like that for weeks before one day she came into the Art Centre, while I finished sketching a drawing I called *Paradise 7*.

Her eyes were crazy, sweat was glistening on her forehead as she marched over to me. She was careful not to move her head while she looked all over the room I couldn't understand why as she knew we were the only ones allowed in here at this time. Her eyes settled on something. I was about to turn my head before she whispered.

"Don't look."

I stopped turning my neck, instead I let me eyes follow her as she got her notebook, and book, and came to sit next to me.

"What are you doing?" I asked as she sat in the chair and started writing something down.

"We need to get out of here," she said, not looking in my direction. "I saw something."
Her voice was so soft as she spoke, like she didn't want someone to hear us.
"What do you mean, you-"
"Shhhhhh, keep it down," she viciously whispered. Her face turned slightly pink. "They are listening, all the time."
"What did you see?" I whispered.
"A few servants were complaining about their living conditions, an-"
"And they should! I saw where they stay and I already spoke to my mother about getting each of them their own bedrooms if that's what this is about, it's being taken care of."
Her face went as white as a sheet.
"What? what's wrong?" I asked.
She couldn't answer me.
"Just tell me," my voice was getting louder.
"They shot the ones who complained, last night."
I didn't know if what she was saying was real or not. It felt like my head was underwater, or like this was a dream.
"Cole, I think they're killing the servants to make your request come true."

CHAPTER 16

AMELIA

The boot opened. A bright light was shining directly into my eyes. I couldn't cover them as my hands were still cuffed behind my back. I squinted before looking away from the light as I felt two hands slip around my waist. I was lifted and tossed over the shoulder of a muscular man in a pure white uniform. I lifted my head to see two more men, in police uniforms walking backwards as they aimed their guns into the street behind us. Blood trickled from my forehead to the ground, and I watched the drops leave a trail like the one I had followed to find the bald man, Cole, and his friends, Rebecca and Brad, before it all went wrong. It was torture to stand so close to the man who had taken away my best friend, and not be able to do anything. It was even worse having to tolerate the extreme idiocy of the fat, egotistic man, Malcolm. A sort of relief washed over me when officer Edward's Ford Focus was rammed into from the side. After the incident there was a silence that led me to believe that maybe my captors were dead. The time that had passed in the room where I found Cole and his friends had calmed me from my initial frenzy. I was chained to the radiator long enough to feel all kinds of emotion as I hated the fact that I admired some of Cole's qualities. It hurt me that the man I hated. The man I hate, was able to make me reconsider my stance toward him in the space of a few hours.

The Cost of Good Intentions

I was placed inside another boot. I couldn't see the make of the car. The man in the uniform took out a syringe with a needle, I started wriggling around, struggling, doing everything I could to make it as hard as possible for him. He put a firm hand on my shoulder before injecting the needle into my neck. Clearing the syringes contents into my body. The boot closed and I was once again plunged into darkness as I felt drowsiness take over before I could no longer stay awake. I woke up to the loud taps of feet meeting concrete before they turned silent as there was the familiar squelch of footsteps navigating damp, grassy terrain. The man who was carrying me stopped walking, I saw a light move past me, from behind my closed eyelids. I heard someone sigh as their knee cracked whilst they crouched down to the ground behind me. There was the sound of fingers clattering against a keypad before a hissing sound. The man who was carrying me continued walking before stopping again a few feet forward. I could see a light grow brighter before I felt someone's cold breath on my face as I felt us begin descending. It was silent in here. The only sounds were the heavy breaths of the man who carried me and the officer behind him. The other officer not joining us. I heard the sound of doors opening. There was a terrible smell when the doors opened. I couldn't control myself. I made a movement that must have been too sudden, and the officer behind me shined the light from his gun directly into my face. The light moved away before I felt a sharp pain in my neck, and I fell asleep again.

I woke to a bright light in a completely white room. The drowsiness was wearing off as I regained control of my body. I was unnervingly hot.

The Cost of Good Intentions

I sat up, taking note that I was in completely white clothing.

The same man who had put me over his shoulder walked into the room carrying a tray with a glass of juice and a plate with avocado on toast. I gulped down the juice before looking at the man, waiting for some sort of indication as to what I was doing here.

He was pleasant as he told me that when I was done getting ready someone was waiting for me, insisting he wasn't allowed to say who as it would ruin a 'special moment', and he wouldn't take me immediately as my host was not ready to receive me. The man told me his name was Elliot, and he had been assigned as my personal servant. He showed me a wardrobe that was built into the wall while he explained his duty to cook, clean, serve and 'pleasure' me, whatever that meant. I was disgusted. It almost felt like a company rebranding. When people actually started to do something about slavery the solution was to just change the word. I didn't know where we were, but I didn't like it.

I looked through the wardrobe, all expensive ugly clothing. I just wanted the clothes I had come in, even though they weren't mine they felt more mine than anything in this wardrobe. I put on the first thing I could find, a green dress with black slip-on shoes. It wasn't important, what was important was finding out who wanted to see me, and for what.

Elliot began knocking on the door, he had knocked once and was surprised when I opened the door as his fist was about to make contact with it once more.

"Let's go, I've waited long enough."

The Cost of Good Intentions

He led me through a maze of corridors before reaching a set of double doors that opened to reveal an Olympic sized pool. We entered the room and walked around the perimeter of the pool through another set of double doors which led to a professional basketball court.

I stopped walking. My body was stiff as I looked at the back of a man. His hair was black and greying at the tips. His stomach a little rounder than the last time I had seen him. He sunk a 3 pointer before he turned around and looked at me. A solid gold watch on his left wrist. A thick chain dangling around his neck across his loose at the chest, tight at the belly style wife beater. His patchy beard perfectly trimmed to make it curve around his plump cheeks. His emerald-green eyes had lines in the corners as a broad smile stretched across his face.

I couldn't contain myself. I just cried. I rushed to him. Embracing him. I squeezed so hard, scared that if I let go he would be gone again. It didn't make sense, but I didn't care. My dad was here, and he would protect me. Whatever was going on wasn't important anymore, because I had got my person back. My hero.

"I can't believe it's you," I sobbed into his chest. "You're actually here."

"I am here my princess," he hugged me, pulling me closer into his chest.

"But how? I thought you were going to get put to sleep."

"It's not important, what's important is that I'm here now, and I'm not going anywhere."

I pulled away as the initial emotion had begun to subside and I started to question how any of it was possible.

"No, I want to know," I said, stepping away from him. "What happened?"

"Maybe it's best if we told you our story together, later…"

"What do you mean, 'we'?"

"I met someone, my princess, she offered me an opportunity," he was still smiling.

My heart was breaking all over again. He looked at me and realised it. He extended his arms, trying to pull me into another hug. I slapped him, as hard as I could. His cheek had a blood red mark across it from the impact. I was going to keep slapping him, to never stop. I was crying uncontrollably when I felt Elliot's firm hands grab hold of me. He was pulling me away. I kicked his shins and dug my nails into his skin, he didn't let go. He carried me out of that room. Away from that monster. I couldn't see anything my vision was blurred from all the tears as Elliot carried me through a series of doors. I continued doing everything I could to get him off me. I felt like I couldn't breathe. He pushed through another set of double doors, and that's when I saw him.

Through my blurred eyes I looked straight at a bald man being pushed in a wheelchair. His hazel eyes were more bloodshot than I'd ever seen them. He didn't slouch in the chair, nor did he sit up perfectly straight. He just stared at me, and our eyes met. I knew the eyes of a broken person when I saw them. One who had lost all purpose. I lost sight of him as I was carried through another set of doors. My sobbing turned to whimpering. The whimpering turned to a small sniffle. My body had lost all energy, I was no longer kicking and screaming. I was limp in Elliot's strong arms when he pushed the door to my room open.

The Cost of Good Intentions

He laid me down gently onto the bed. My eyes lazily closed as I didn't even have the strength to put the blanket over me. That is what it felt like to lose a hero.

The next time I got woken up, the same procedure occurred. I met my dad at the basketball court, but he wasn't alone today. A woman with short grey hair stood next to him. She jokingly swooned every time he hit a bucket. He laughed as he kissed his muscles each time he did. The wound was still raw from the last time we spoke. It hurt to look at him smiling and genuinely having a good time when I was falling apart. Did he even care when he left?

The door swung shut behind me as Elliot let it go, whilst he stayed outside of the room.

The sound echoed across the court and alerted them to my presence.

"Amelia, my sweetheart," my dad said to me, pretending that I hadn't slapped his still-red cheek. "I would like you to meet someone very special to me, this is my wife, and president, of Clayland, Eleanor Clay," he said her name like a TV presenter, hyping up a crowd before some big celebrity enters the stage.

"It's so lovely to meet you, Amelia! We are going to do our best to make sure that Clayland is perfect for you!" she spoke like she was selling something to you or pitching something to a board of potential investors. Who was this woman? What opportunity did she offer my dad?

"Can we talk… alone?" I looked from my dad to Eleanor.

"Why of course," Eleanor said, her voice smiling more than her face, "remember, if there's anything you need, don't be shy to ask!" she exited the court from another door on the side of the court.

"Please just tell me what is going on here, dad," I fought back tears.

His smile faded as he looked at me. A sad look taking over. "Sit down, my girl," he walked over to the empty bleachers and took a seat.

I sat next to him.

He sighed before he began.

"I was dying, each day it was getting a little harder to breath. The things that I could once do so effortlessly were no longer possible. I could feel my body was riddled with the cancer, and you know I had accepted my fate. But everything changed. I watched you grow, and develop into this kind, beautiful, caring woman. I saw so much of your mother in you. It broke my heart that I wouldn't get to see any more of it. One day I was walking in town, and I saw Eleanor. Her head was down, looking at a thick bunch of papers. She wasn't paying attention; she was about to walk into the street and a bus was coming. I grabbed her wrist and made sure she didn't walk into the street. When she realized what she was about to do she wanted to thank me by taking me for a coffee. I told her all about you and our situation and it turned out that Eleanor knew a lot of wealthy people. She offered to help me, and even pay for treatment that had a hundred percent success rate. I took her offer, and it wasn't long until I was cancer free. I was going to tell you, but she said I couldn't, and I could tell she meant it. Something like that gets out and everyone will want it, but this wasn't something that could be widely distributed. I liked spending time with Eleanor, so we carried on seeing each other and we fell in love. Then one day we were sitting inside her apartment when she told me that one of her environmentalist friends told her the planet was dying. On the brink of collapse. She told me that she had a friend who was building something, for when it started to happen, but everyone had to pay for their place. I didn't have the money to pay for you, and Eleanor could only pay for me and her, but I knew that my chances of getting the money to pay for you would be better if I was fully involved. It was only recently that Eleanor became president, when her friend passed away."

I listened to him, hanging on every word, wanting him to say one thing that I could grasp on to. I wanted his cape to return, and to feel the warmth that I associated with his memory. Because that's what I remembered about him, always. He put me before himself, because that's what parents do, but the more he went on, the more I realized how wrong my interpretation of him had been. I was an afterthought, and maybe I was selfish in wanting him to stay, but after years of homelessness, with Rory, my perspective had changed. The whole concept of this place was selfish in nature, who gave anyone the power to decide who lives and who dies when catastrophe strikes? It made no sense, Ben Clark, a cancer riddled middle aged man meets the right person at the right time and boom, he is saved. All because someone had the money to pay for him. Apart from being a great dad, up until a point, he was not exceptional by nature. He had no natural talents or honed skills, the only thing that had developed in my absence was his greed, and that seemed to be a requirement of being a resident in Clayland.

"So that's it? You just left me to fend for yourself?"

The Cost of Good Intentions

"Swee-"

"No! don't call me that! You left me! Do you know how hard these years have been for me? Do you know the pain I felt every year when the day that you left me comes around? I was scared, and lost, and you left me when you had another option!"

"What option! There were no other options!" he raised his voice.

"Of course there were! You could have stayed and taken care of me. You could have taken me to school, and brushed my hair, and read me books as I fell asleep. We could have gone to theme parks all across the country and ate all the iced cream and candy floss they had in each one. Instead, you chose to indulge in some bullshit world that doesn't mean anything. You had a choice to tell the world about this place, instead you kept quiet and let them know that you valued your life more than everyone else's. So don't try to pretend this is about me, because you don't get to leave my life as a victim and return as a hero when you're responsible for all the pain in between."

"And to what end, Amelia? People live, and people die, I saved who I could save. I don't write the rules, I don't have the power to change them, I can just play my hand the best way I know how. I did this for us, I don't know how you can't see that. Should I not eat because there isn't enough food to go around?"

"Well, it looks like you're eating for two."

"It may seem like that but old age makes the body behave differently."

We both went silent, looking out at the court in front of us. I felt hopelessness. Not sure what the entire point was anymore. The way he described it, there was nothing outside of Clayland now. Where there was once an entire planet, there was now darkness, emptiness.

"I'm not a bad man, Amelia," his voice back to normal volume, "Each part of this place was designed to make life here more enjoyable than anything you could experience on Earth; anything you could experience in Nod. We have the facilities to sustain us for years to come, without labour, without hardship. Before yesterday I dreamed of the day when we would be reunited, and I could spend each day with you. I've already picked out a selection of books for you to read, my personal favourites, and thought about each activity we would do while we grow older. So, please, just give it a chance."

I didn't say anything. I was contemplating everything he had said. There was a general empathy in the way he said it. I had learned over the last few days that raw emotion is often misleading. I wanted to give myself the time to think about all he'd said, and I told him as much before I stood up and started walking to the door.

"Take the time you need," he said, "but on Friday you're going to be expected in a room that Elliot will escort you to. It's a promise I made to Eleanor."

"Why do I need to be there?"

"She wants you to meet her son, so that we could maybe start to grow, as a family."

I wanted to vomit.

"I need you to be prepared though," his voice was stern.

"For what?"

"For her son being Cole Clay."

CHAPTER 17

I spent days in my room. After a few hours of sitting and going over the conversation with my dad I eventually exhausted all of my energy in trying to figure out what to do next. Whenever I had felt this way in the past there was always one thing that I was able to do to take my mind off of things and in the process, get a different perspective. I rang the bell that Elliot had left on the table in my room. It sickened me to do it, but I didn't know anything about Clayland. He appeared in my room shortly after, his hulk-like figure filled up the entirety of the door frame.
"Could you please bring me a book, Elliot?"
"Do you have a preference, Ms Clark?"
"No, just the first one you come across."
He left the room and came back a few moments later with a pristine copy of *To Kill a Mockingbird*.
I sat and read the book through a single sit in before spending the next days deep in thought and going through a circular rhythm of sleeping, eating, bathing and repeating the process. It was so hard to determine the time in Clayland, there was no indication that time was passing at all. The only way to really keep track was to separate the days into the three meals that largely stuck to the same formats of breakfast, lunch and dinner as you would on Earth. The absence of a clock would have been unsettling had it not worked in my favour as I had no distractions when sorting through my emotions. Elliot told me that it was Friday, and time to prepare for my meeting with Cole Clay, his mother and my dad.

The Cost of Good Intentions

I wore a sundress with sunflowers that were scattered all over.

I was escorted to a room through a series of doors, each of the rooms had different species. The first was a room with different birds, the second was a room with land animals and the third was filled with aquatic animals.

I reached out to touch the glass as I saw a clownfish swim toward it. Elliot noticed and he suddenly panicked.

"Don't touch the glass," he grabbed my hand, a bit too desperately. Realising that he had, he gently let it go again. "The uhh… The sound attracts the sharks and I'm a bit scared of them."

It seemed like an odd explanation considering that he knew there was no way they could physically reach us. I decided to just listen to him, it would be easier to move forward if I didn't go around making enemies.

We then entered a room with a monument in the corner, a light was shining directly onto it. A stone bench was in the middle of the room. My dad and Eleanor were already in the room, looking out a glass window that overlooked an extremely green field. They turned to smile at me when I entered the room.

"Thank you for joining us, Amelia," Eleanor had a bright smile on her face as she said it. "Hopefully Cole won't be too long."

My dad walked over to me, giving me a kiss on the forehead, "Thank you for doing this for me, sweetheart."

I let him because I still wasn't sure what the best way forward was.

"What is that?" I asked, walking towards the monument.

The Cost of Good Intentions

"That is our Wall of Sacrifice," Eleanor walked to stand beside me. "It has the names of all the people who have lost their lives during the creation of Clayland, it is important we remember the sacrifices that a brave few have made so that we are able to live in this paradise," she said it like a campaign speech, looking from the monument to my dad, the smile on her face even larger. I read the names, each of them were unfamiliar to me, but one stuck out like a sore thumb. It was written so small.

Elon Gatner.

I wasn't sure if it was the same Elon that we were on the way to go rescue, but the name Elon was so uncommon that I couldn't help but think that it was.

This could be the *same* Elon that apparently started all of this. A lot of things were falling into place, all at once. My dad had said that the original creator of this place had passed away and that's why Eleanor had taken over. He didn't say *how* he had passed though.

Did they plan this?

Did they plan to kill Elon so they could take over?

I didn't want to believe it.

My head was spinning so I went to go sit on the bench. I started to cry a little bit. I was so scared and confused.

"Sweetheart, what's wrong?" My dad rested his hand on my left shoulder.

"Sorry," I sniffled as I wiped my eyes with the back of my hands. "This is all just very overwhelming."

"It's okay, take your time, we have plenty of it," he said softly.

It was so hard to consider that this man who was so tender in that moment could be capable of something so evil. It was almost unthinkable, to the point that I felt guilty even having the thought.

"Is this about Cole? Do you want us to reschedule, because we can do that if you like?" Eleanor said, now standing by my right shoulder.

"No, that's okay," I said as I wiped the last of my tears.

I actually wanted to see Cole now. I needed to see if he was involved, because if he wasn't then he and I were probably the only two people in Clayland that didn't have a clue about Elon's murder.

I felt my dad move his hand off of my shoulder, him and Eleanor walked back toward the window and continued looking out while deep in conversation.

Literal seconds later Cole walked into the room from the opposite direction I had come.

He looked worse than I had ever seen him. His bald head was shining with the formation of new sweat. His hands trembled terribly as he observed me with his manic hazel eyes that were so red it looked like the white didn't exist. A gold watch, just like the one my dad wore, was on his left wrist which already made me question where his loyalties lie. I sat and stared at the blank wall ahead of me as I saw Eleanor and my dad turn in complete synchronicity with duplicate smiles on their faces. It all seemed like one giant charade that had been rehearsed a thousand times over.

Cole spoke to his mother, asking about his friend Rebecca and his old boss Malcolm. I suddenly wanted to check the Wall of Sacrifice for their names but thought against it as I didn't want to raise any unnecessary suspicion. He spoke to her in a way that no son would talk to a mother if they were on good terms, but with all that had happened I was still hesitant to trust him. I had misjudged the character of someone so close to me, someone that I thought I knew more than anyone, so who's to say that Cole Clay, whom I only met a few days ago, through less than favourable happenings, could not trick me into confiding in him when he has been in on this whole operation with his mother all along?

And how was it that they seemed to know the exact moment that Cole would walk into the room?

There were too many coincidental circumstances to ignore. I tensed when Eleanor and my dad revealed their request for me and Cole to spend time together in an Art Centre. On one hand I thought that maybe they were genuine and actually wanted us to bond, on another I thought that this was their way of keeping tabs on me to make sure their subtle indoctrination was working as I spent more time in Clayland.

Whatever their intentions were was irrelevant, because the only person who I was interested in right now was Cole.

He tried to refuse but Eleanor was insistent, and as she finished speaking my dad cleared his throat and Elliot opened the door to lead us to the Art Centre. I walked ahead of Cole, to see if he would try to catch up to me and make small talk. He didn't, so I stayed in front of him all the way through a maze of corridors before, finally, Elliot opened a door and stepped aside to give me access into a room.

I stopped when I entered.

For all the lack of colour present in the rest of Clayland, this one room was so vibrant and full of colour that it seemed all of the colour from everywhere else had been sucked into it. Bookshelves lined the right-hand side walls from floor to ceiling with their shelves filled with high profile titles *Jane Eyre, Far From the Madding Crowd* and *All the Bright Places* catching my attention. The left-hand side of the room had a selection of the world's most valuable art. The middle had a huge table that stretched all the way to the far end of the room. 20 chairs surrounded the table, each neatly tucked in.

There was a sketchpad with different kinds of paints, and brushes, and pencils sitting in front of one of the seats on the table. In front of the seat next to it was a notebook with a pen on top of it, beside a copy *A Tale of Two Cities*. I picked up the notebook, pen, and copy of the novel and went to sit at the farthest possible point from Cole. I needed to study him, make sure he could be trusted.

I opened the book and stared at a blank page. I sat like that for a while, thinking about everything, not able to write a single thing down in fear that it would be taken and used to try get a gauge on my headspace. I was thankful when Elliot opened the door and told us that our time was up for the day, I was less thankful when he told me that it was to be a regular arrangement.

I was instructed to go to the Art Centre every day. I didn't argue, just followed the instructions, following Elliot every day as he escorted me. I used the time to think about a plan I was making. Elliot had become more relaxed around me; I didn't catch him sneaking quick glances to see where I was behind him. He got to a point where he left me behind in one of the corridors, by accident. I stopped to tie the laces of the black sneakers I had been wearing for the last couple of weeks, and he just carried on walking. I stood there until he came running back. Sweat dripped off of him, and he was breathless as he apologised for leaving me behind. He had taken quite a long time to figure out that he had left me behind though, which gave me an idea. It had been eating away at me how scared he looked when I was going to touch the glass in the sea-life section, there was something there that they didn't want me to know. So, I was patient and waited again for when he would become more relaxed. Then one day I silently stopped walking and watched him continue walking, towards the maze of corridors that led to the Art Centre. As he rounded the corner, and I was out of his sight, I started running toward the sea-life display. I was careful to keep my footsteps as silent as I could before I knew I would be out of earshot. I made it into the display and pressed the glass.

The glass was not glass.

I watched as the display on the giant monitor that has been projecting sea life changed to various images of all the different rooms in Clayland.

I saw a room that looked like a beach, the basketball court, all the corridors. I took note that there was a blind spot near the bathroom facilities in each of our rooms. Every room was being monitored.

I quickly pressed the screen again and the pictures of the exact same clown fish I had seen before returned. I rushed back to the corridor where Elliot had left me, and immediately got down on my knee and pretended to tie my shoe. I struggled to control my breath but managed to do so before Elliot came rushing around the corner, breathlessly.

"Sorry, Elliot, needed to tie my shoe," I said as I gave him the best smile I could manage.

He put his hands on his hips as he struggled to catch his breath, while he looked at me with a frown on his face. I think he was sceptical, but he didn't have enough reason to doubt me before he told me it was okay, and I knew that I wouldn't be able to do that again.

I followed him to the Art Centre, taking my usual seat at the opposite end of the table to Cole.

He didn't look at me, he was too fixated on something he was busy drawing.

I did my best to be discreet as I watched him. It was the best he had looked since I had met him. He no longer sweated randomly, and his hazel eyes had regained their milk white backdrop.

I watched him groan as he looked at his watch, before Elliot came in and announced that our time was up for the day.

Cole was the first to leave, I told Elliot to just give me a moment to pick out a book. I picked up the copy of *The Tale of Two Cities* and I purposefully walked the long way around the desk as I wanted to see what was in Cole's sketchbook. Elliot's eyes followed me, but he didn't say a word. Probably delighted with the fact he would have something to report to his self-deemed superiors.

I opened the page and flicked through a plethora of sketches, starting with the image of a man with a sad face who was being pulled in two directions. On his left side was the image of a person with a happy face. Their pockets were turned outwards to display that they were empty. The man who was being pulled had only his left pocket turned

The Cost of Good Intentions

outwards to match that of the person on the left. On the right-hand side was a person with an angry face, but their pockets were overflowing with money, to match that of the right pocket of the man being pulled.

His most recent drawing was extremely different to his first one. At the top was the word *Paradise 7* which was a drawing that was an exact replica of one of the rooms in Clayland.

The journey told a story, a story of him being slowly convinced that this place is anything but a den of the worst that humanity has to offer.

I closed the sketch pad and walked to the bookshelf. I picked up two books from the shelf, I didn't even look at the cover of one as I pulled it from the shelf and replaced it with the book I had brought. The second book I picked up was a copy of *Animal farm* by George Orwell. I left it on top of his sketchbook and walked out of the Art Centre, following Elliot all the way back to my room.

I was sick of everything in Clayland, I didn't want any part of it. Whatever this place was, it wasn't for me. So, the next day when Elliot came to collect me and take me to the Art Centre, I refused, requesting for books to be brought from the library for me to read in the comfort of my bed. That day extended to weeks, and in turn months. My dad had been steering clear of me, hoping that if he gave me time, I would be more willing to embrace the things he wanted me to embrace.

Spending all that time alone, reflecting on being a watched prisoner threw me into an unmatched depression. A depression that wilted and made way to a spark. I had been hopeless for quite some time before I fought internally and came to the conclusion that the only way I would improve my circumstance was by doing something other than sitting in the same four walls and hoping that everything would somehow change.

Elliot woke me one morning with the usual tray of breakfast and juice, he had already turned to leave when I caught his attention.

I cleared my throat, "Elliot, could I go see my dad please?" He was more than happy to satisfy my request, possibly thinking that that was me now taking the time to extend an olive branch to my dad, and he would somehow get rewarded from it.

I was taken to my dad who was in his usual place being the basketball court, he dribbled the ball before body checking a tall slender man in a pure white uniform and running in for an easy lay-up. I found it sad that it seemed like he spent a lot of time here and would never be able to compete against anyone other than a servant who was clearly too terrified to hurt his fragile ego.

"Did you see that, sweetheart?" my dad jogged to the side-lines to be handed a towel and a bottle of water by another servant.

"Like watching Jordan," I mumbled as I walked toward him.

"What's that?" he wiped the sweat from his forehead.

"I said that was impressive," I gave him a fake smile.

"Thanks, sweety. Anyway, what did you want to talk about? Are you feeling alright?"

"Yes dad, everything is fine," I lied. "I just wanted to spend more time with you, to try make up for lost time. I feel like I haven't really seen all that Clayland has to offer, could I get a tour?"

He looked mildly surprised but seemed to embrace this apparent change in my approach to life in this hellhole.

"Of course, sweetheart. Well, what are you in the mood for? We have anything you can think of here."

"I'm not sure, maybe you could just take me around to have a look at all the facilities, and I'll tell you if there is something that I like."

So that's what we did. He walked me around the entirety of Clayland. Explaining how long each section had taken to make. They had created one giant replica of every leisurely activity you could think of on Earth. Each room held different appeal and brought a different atmosphere to life. Each detail was precise and purposeful to try its best to recreate the same wow factor you would experience when standing in front of something as monumental as the Pyramids of Giza. It was an ironic comparison considering that when I asked who built the structures in the rooms, I was told that almost everything had been built by the servants in Clayland, with a few dying during the time of their construction and having their names inscribed on the Wall of Sacrifice. While I did get a sense of awe as we walked through all the different rooms, I couldn't help but notice the lack of people, in a good portion of the rooms there were only about 5 or 6 people, even though the room was designed and capable of holding more. Even as we walked through the corridors where names were printed on the doors of the rooms, the corridors were hauntingly empty.

The Cost of Good Intentions

It wasn't until we reached a room I had seen on the cameras, which was a recreation of a standard beach, that I saw people. Laughter and chatter filled the room from corner to corner, but the volume of their voices decreased when they were alerted to our presence. I noticed the quick glances in our direction, and the way my dad stood straighter in front of them as we continued to walk through the room. I looked up at an incredibly blue sky which held a blazing sun. Looking at the sun I took notice of the climate for the first time since I had been in Clayland. Walking in that room was like walking in any other, no matter where we had been before that the temperature was constant. It should have been hotter in there, all things considered, but it seemed that the whole of Clayland's weather was artificial.

"This room is the busiest room in Clayland as it was included in the cheapest package when we rolled out the project plans."

I struggled to hide my disgust.

As we walked through the room, I noticed someone was staring at me with a look of malice, it made me uncomfortable, but not as uncomfortable as when I noticed my dad staring back at him with a look that was definitely a warning.

We walked through another set of doors, leaving the beach room behind, and entered the Monument room.

"Well, you've seen all of Clayland," he seemed like he was in a rush suddenly, I couldn't tell if it was because he was thinking about the man who had been staring at me in the beach room.

The Cost of Good Intentions

"I'll get Elliot to escort you back to the Art Centre, that's all the time I have today, my sweetheart," he was already walking back towards the beach room.

Elliot wordlessly walked to the door leading to the displays to hold it open for me. I sighed as I started walking toward him.

But then another door opened, one that I hadn't seen in the far end of the room. I watched as a woman wearing the same white uniform as Elliot walked into the Monument room.

She was startled when she saw us, but she carried on walking all the way through the door that Elliot held open. I couldn't help but notice that Elliot had the same look of panic that he had when I tried to touch the 'glass'. The look was gone in a flash as he cleared his throat.

"Come, Ms Clark, we need to go to the Art Centre."

They didn't want me to know what was behind that door. I needed to find a way to get there, without being spied on. I told Elliot that I didn't feel well, and I didn't want to go to the Art Centre. He reluctantly took me back to my room when he had no other option because of my adamant refusal.

When I got to my room, I laid on the bed, and tried to devise a plan to get access into that room. I was only interrupted, what felt like, a few hours later, when Elliot's usual knock sounded before he entered my room with dinner. Rice and steak with the customary orange juice which was naturally included with every meal.

I brought the juice to my lips before stopping just short as another realization had dawned upon me.

The Cost of Good Intentions

Every day since I had been there, I had felt an ease wash over me not long after dinner time. I would easily drift off to sleep, waking up to Elliot bringing in breakfast. Without knowing the time, it was hard to discern at what point I was falling asleep, but up until that point I had assumed that life in Clayland was naturally following the same schedule I had for years. That I was falling asleep at 22:00 and Elliot was waking me at 6:00.

It was only after I was given the tour and noting that each room's temperature was regulated that I noticed that it seemed to be hotter in the evenings. I thought about how easily I was falling asleep.

I took the cup of juice and casually walked to the bathroom, pretending to take sips of the juice along the way. When I reached the blind spot I spat the juice into the toilet, pouring the rest of the glass in and flushing. I went to the tap and washed my hands, looking into the mirror I pretended to observe myself, and then I saw the smallest red dot. That was where the camera was.

I summoned Elliot, telling him I wasn't hungry. He noted the empty glass and didn't complain as he took the plate full of food away with the empty glass.

I sat on the bed, waiting to see if my usual tiredness might take hold, but it never did.

It wasn't long before something strange happened. Something that hadn't happened since I came to Clayland. I closed my eyes, feigning exhaustion, I kept my brain alert so I wouldn't fall asleep, and then out of nowhere.

The lights turned off, and I was plunged into darkness.

CHAPTER 18

My eyes shot open; the darkness was so thick you couldn't see anything. The red dot was easily visible.

I heard a sound come from the corridors that normally maintained a perfect silence. I heard the shuffling of feet, and low whispers as multiple shadowy figures passed my door before I saw a flash of light.

The light reminded me of the one that the officer had pointed in my face all those months ago, and I realized that someone was leading multiple people down the corridor at gunpoint.

I was hesitant, I didn't want to move in case the camera had night vision, and someone was watching, but I couldn't just sit there. I tried to comfort myself by reasoning that nobody should be watching because they thought we were all asleep. It was the only hopeful thought I could muster, so I clung onto it as I got out of the bed and silently walked to the door.

When I entered the corridor, I looked left, the direction that the people were walking, and saw the man with the gun turning the corner into one of the other corridors. The corridors were the same kind of dark that I remember from my last day in Nod. It wasn't as thick as it was in the bedrooms.

I stayed low, keeping my footsteps quiet as I followed the group through the series of corridors before I watched them enter the double doors that led to the swimming pool.

The Cost of Good Intentions

I peeped through the keyhole of the doors to see six people in pure white uniforms standing side-by-side staring at the blue water ahead as the man holding the gun stood behind them and aimed at them. I watched as Eleanor walked into the room from the basketball court, followed by my dad.

"It has been brought to my attention that the six of you have been negligent in your duties to the paying residents here in Clayland. It pains me to know that after I saved you from the literal apocalypse you would spit in my face by complaining to the residents about your living conditions. Your lack of appreciation to be afforded the opportunity to be the servants of pioneers of the New Age is sickening. You are here by merit. Allowed to be here at all from the kindness of my heart," Eleanor pretended to wipe away tears, "But you have killed the last bit of good in me, and I cannot allow you to unsettle the rest of the residents and servants, so you must be examples.

Examples of what happens when you take advantage of my grace," She started crying as she threw herself into my dad's arms. He held her close to his chest as he looked away.

The man with the gun shot each of the six in the back. Their bodies fell into the pool and the blue transformed to red.

I covered my mouth with my hand. Fighting back tears of my own. My breath was trembling, as I turned around and ran back to my room. It was so hard not to make a sound.

When I reached my room, I closed the door before I rushed to climb into the bed, threw my head into my pillow and screamed.

The Cost of Good Intentions

The next day Elliot woke me up. He put the back of his hand on my head. I felt terrible. I was sweating profusely. My stomach was aching, and my head was throbbing. I had never taken drugs before, I'd never even had a drink, but I knew this was the withdrawal from whatever they had been putting in my orange juice to make me go to sleep. My hair was matted and stuck to my forehead.

"Do you want some medicine Ms Clark?"

"No, that's alright Elliot, I think I am passed the worst of it."

"Are you sure? Because you look terrible," his voice held a genuine concern, and I was grateful for that, but I still wasn't sure I actually liked Elliot.

From the first day I was there he had unsettled me by not really hiding the fact that one of his duties was to observe me at all possible times. I had fallen so deeply into the monotonous routine in Clayland that it became second nature to consider him the same way a person might consider their shadow. It was quite apparent to me that at every moment those lights were on he was never further than a few moments away, and Clayland wasn't a small place. What could the incentive be to work so tirelessly and never once break character? It bothered me that I watched him keep the same neutral expression throughout the day, no matter when I saw him. He never showed any indication of fatigue or emotion, bar the two occasions where he feared he had neglected his duties, and the few when he thought of his reward for new information, he would present Eleanor and my dad. I thought of Rory for the first time in a while. He would have hated everything about Elliot. He would have hated the fact that Elliot seemed to willingly conform to being exploited, considering all the knowledge I have now, but maybe it was Rory's absence that allowed me to question my rationale in the absence of my normal routine of listening intently to his soliloquies on the moral injustice of conforming to modern day tyrants.

Maybe I had just grown soft, but I couldn't deny my feeling of admiration for Elliot, there was an element of nobility in knowing that he was probably aware of his unfavourable circumstances, but bravely endured them for an unknown, yet highly desirable reward.

"I just want to get back to my reading, Elliot."

"I'll go get you a book from the Art Centre, Ms Clark."

"No, it's alright, I haven't been to the Art Centre for a while now and I want to go."

Elliot's eyes lit up ever so slightly as he would once again have something, 'positive' to report.

I got ready, still fully feeling the effects of withdrawal. I couldn't not go, I needed to see Cole who, up until that point, hadn't given me any reason not to trust him. I had asked about him over the course of my self-isolation, just out of curiosity, and I was told he had been in the Art Centre every day since my departure.

When I entered the Art Centre. I made sure not to move my head as I scanned the room for the camera. It was hard to spot as my attention kept getting drawn to new pieces of art and the bookshelves that were now completely filled. My eyes settled on the tiny red dot in one of the corners. I saw Cole start to turn his head to see if he could identify what I was looking at.

"Don't look," I whispered, and he stopped turning his head.

Keeping its location in mind I got the notebook and pen, that still sat exactly where I left it, and placed them in the space in front of the chair right next to Cole as I sat down. His eyes followed me as I opened my notebook and began writing him a note, making sure that his back covered the notepad.

"What are you doing?"

"We need to get out of here," I said, not looking in his direction. "I saw something."

"What do you mean, you – "

"Shhhhhh, keep it down," I viciously whispered. "They are listening, all the time."

"Who's they? What did you see?" he whispered. There was something *off* about him.

"Our parents. A few servants were complaining about their living conditions, an-"

"And they should! I saw where they stay and I already spoke to my mother about getting each of them their own bedrooms if that's what this is about, it's being taken care of."

My body felt cold. I didn't know if I should tell him. He wasn't in some alliance with Eleanor and my dad. He wanted to help the servants.

"What's wrong?" he asked.

I couldn't answer him.

"Just tell me," his voice was getting louder.

"They shot the ones who complained, last night." I whispered.

I was going to be sick.

"Cole, I think they're killing the servants to make your request come true."

His expression didn't change.

I drew his attention to read what I wrote.

Do you know Elon Gatner? Blink twice if yes. Was written neatly across the top of the page.

I watched as he looked down at the notepad with a confused expression. Cole and I needed to spend some time alone. The bodies of those six had to be somewhere, and there wasn't any indication that they were still in Clayland. There was only one area that I hadn't been in the whole of Clayland, Cole had been, but the look Elliot had on his face when he realized I knew about a door that wasn't supposed to be seen by me was unmistakable. Cole must have missed something. There was something in there that they didn't want us to see, and we needed to find out what it was.

"What area is your room close to?" I whispered as I ripped the page from the notepad, crumpling it up and sticking it in the pocket of my blue jeans.

He didn't answer, his face was still expressionless as he thought about what I just told him.

"Cole!" I whispered a bit louder.

"S… sorry. This is all just a bit much."

He didn't seem like he was aware what was going on around him. His face twitched at random intervals, and I realised that they were probably drugging him more heavily than they were me.

"Cole, you need to stop drinking the juice, they are putting something into it."

The Cost of Good Intentions

"No, that can't be true, my mom has worked hard to get me sober," his pupils were dilated, and he talked slower than any sober person would, his words not slurring but they didn't have the same sharpness as regular speech.
"Cole, I am telling you just stop drinking it and you will see what I am talking about."
He still looked like I was speaking another language. This was pointless. He needed to get off the drugs they were feeding him if he was going to be any help.
"Just think about it," I whispered before I stood and walked out the room. I told Elliot I didn't feel well. He didn't complain considering I was still sweating, badly.

Over the course of the next few days, I went to the Art Centre, much to the delight of Elliot because each day I took note that he watched me sit next to Cole, and he took that as a sign that our relationship was improving. Our conversations were one sided, and limited, as each day we whispered, and it seemed like Cole had no recollection of our conversations from the previous days. I was recovering from the initial withdrawal of the drug infused orange juice that I still received on a nightly basis. It had become a part of my routine to regularly hold big portions of the juice in my mouth before making it to the toilet and spitting it out. Every night they marched new servants passed my bedroom door, which made me hesitant to try go to the servant's quarters in the evenings. I hated to think about it, but I realized how badly I needed Cole. There was no chance for me to get into the servant's quarters in the day, I was watched too closely. I needed someone to keep watch in the evening as I tried to find out what was going on. Cole seemed to be worsening day-by-day though, his looks of confusion intensified as he spiralled deeper into his unknown addiction. I had thought about leaving him to continue in his dazed confusion, because he looked quite content to sit and fill his days recreating different versions of the same drawing. My patience grew thin, and I was already thinking of ways to get into the servant's quarters without him when I wondered how any mother could sit back and let her son get drugged, all so she could hide her ugly secrets in the dark of night, but it was so clear to see, even from the only conversation that I had witnessed between the two of them, that Cole posed a threat to her, because he didn't agree with her and she didn't want anyone to know it. She had brought him here to shine a light on herself as a motherly figure, but it suited her just fine that he was comatose, away from prying eyes. The Art Centre had been reserved for a reason; nobody ever saw us for a reason. It gave our parents exactly what they craved. They got to keep up their image without any effort whatsoever. It was why my dad was so glad to walk me around, loudly explaining all the, 'incredible' things that Clayland has to offer. I was as much his prized pony as Cole was his mothers.

I was once alone, and afraid, and Rory had saved me from that. He had put his arm around me and guided me, protecting me from all the bad things and all the bad people. That kind of compassion was exactly what Clayland lacked. Everyone had their own personal motivations for being here and, apart from us, they had paid to be here. They wanted this. We weren't given the choice. I was fighting for my choice, while I watched Cole get his forcefully taken away without him even realizing it.

The Cost of Good Intentions

If I had gone into that orphanage my life would have been so different, and I don't think it would have been for the better, but Rory taught me that I still had a choice, even if I was scared, it was still there. I wanted to do the same for Cole, because I wouldn't be any different to anyone in Clayland if I looked at this injustice and turned the other way knowing that I could have done something that would make a difference.

One day I walked into the Art Centre and realized that Cole wasn't there. He was always the first one in. I furrowed my brow as I took a seat in my new normal seat. I spent the afternoon reading but found myself unable to concentrate as I wondered where he was.

He didn't come to the Art Centre for the rest of the week. I asked Elliot where he was, and Elliot told me that Cole wasn't feeling well. I panicked as a pang of guilt rested in my stomach as I asked myself if I could have done more to help him.

The first good news since I had been in Clayland was brought about when one day, several weeks later, Cole was sitting at his seat when I walked into the Art Centre. It looked like he was studying the images in his sketchpad, like he didn't recognize any of them.

His eyes had red rings around them like he had been crying recently.

I sat next to him, picking up my copy of *Dear Martin* and opened to the page I had got to the day before.

I noticed that Cole had taken off his gold watch, he was silent for most of the time as he continued to look at each variation of *Paradise* In his sketchpad. Toward the end of our allocated time, he opened up my notepad and wrote.

The Cost of Good Intentions

Why did you ask about Elon?

I took the pen, my hands trembled as I wrote.

Your mom and my dad had him killed.

A single tear fell down his cheek.

"I'm in the straight corridor two doors away from the beach."

I knew the one.

Finally, I had someone with me.

CHAPTER 19

The lights went out and I carefully listened for the fresh batch of servants being led to their slaughter. When they passed, I got out of the bed and made my way to the corridors.

I had mapped out the path in my head, crouching and checking the corners as I carefully navigated each corridor until I finally arrived at the door with Cole's name on it. I opened the door and slipped inside, unable to see anything again.

"Cole," I whispered, "are you awake?"

It took a moment and then he asked me,

"What's going on in this place? I'm just confused, everything is such a blur, I'm not even sure why you're speaking to me when last thing I remember is that you wanted to kill me because I-"

"Don't."

If he said it I would break again. I could feel the rage bubbling, daring one thing to tip it over. I couldn't hate him right now. I couldn't occupy my time thinking about what he took from me. It had taken a lot for some part of me to forgive him, but I could still feel the part of me that wanted to make him pay. I couldn't afford to have my head cloudy, and that's what that kind of hate does. It takes away your ability to see anything else. It doesn't care about the how's or the why's, it just cares about fulfilling itself.

I took a deep breath to calm myself.

The Cost of Good Intentions

"I'm not going to pretend I like it, but I have no other choice. I need you to keep watch while I find out what they're hiding in the servant's quarters."

It took me by surprise when I heard him start to cry.

"It's all my fault, I should have just kept quiet, they're dead because of me."

"No," I whispered. "No, Cole, it isn't your fault. You stood up for them, you tried to help them."

"They would still be here if I didn't say anything."

"You can't take responsibility for that. You aren't responsible for anyone else's actions, Cole. Your intention was good."

"Intention? Good intention means nothing. It doesn't change the reality of what happened."

"You're wrong. Good intention means everything, it only means nothing when you don't perform the action to back it up."

I heard him calm down.

"Let's go to the servants' quarters."

We walked through two doors before we entered the beach area. When we opened the doors, we both stood as we looked up at the sky. The room no longer had the sun, in its place was a cloudless, dark sky that was an exact copy of the one we last saw in Nod. Cole and I continued to the Monument room, walking silently to the door that led to the servants' quarters.

It was strange to be in this room when the light didn't shine directly onto the Wall of Sacrifice. I wanted to be as quick as possible, but Cole had diverted his route. He was now standing directly in front of the Wall of Sacrifice as he read the list of names. No doubt looking for one name in particular. I stood next to him as he found it, he just stared at it.

I didn't know Cole very well, but I could relate to what he was feeling. I knew what it was like to stand there and feel like you were incomplete. I knew how he was suffering, and having wanted nothing but for him to suffer from the moment I met him I suddenly wanted to take all his pain away.

While we stood and stared at the Wall of Sacrifice time seemed to stand still. The room was so silent and still as we mentally paid our respect to everyone on that monument, because they were human and had had their lives stolen.

The silence was broken when we heard voices approaching from one of the corridors. I didn't want to take the risk of going into the servants' quarters when I was aware that that was the likely destination of the people that approached.

I pulled Cole behind the Wall of Sacrifice, in the hopes that it would do an adequate job of concealing us.

The voices of my dad and Eleanor were clearly audible when they entered the Monument room.

It was easy to tell that they weren't alone, the sound of multiple footsteps echoed throughout the room. The footsteps ceased and the room was silent again until the door shut.

"Put them in the cage with the others," my father's voice was stern as he gave the command.

 I covered my mouth with my hand in an attempt to silence my breath which had become more erratic as time went on. I heard movement before the doors to the servants' quarters opened. I looked at Cole, his expression was blank again. I looked at what he was looking at. I hadn't realized that the Wall of Sacrifice was double sided. There were names all along the back of it as well, I read them and realized why Cole was staring at it so intently. In the middle of the right-hand side column were the names.

Rebecca Kelser

Malcolm Myers

I watched as Cole left the safety of our hiding place and charged straight for Eleanor and my father. Before he could reach them he was tackled to the ground by Elliot.

They knew we were there all along.

Two officers picked me up from behind the Wall of Sacrifice. I kicked and screamed as they put me on the ground next to Cole. He glared up at Elliot, before an officer kicked him in the face. He was knocked unconscious instantly. I looked up at my father and Eleanor and then at Elliot.

"You are fucking monsters," I gritted my teeth.

The same officer who had kicked Cole stood in front of me now.

I watched as he lifted his foot and brought it down as hard as he could.

CHAPTER 20

COLE

I couldn't focus on anything but the smell when I woke up in. It was so strong that even when I covered my nose little bits of it slipped through the smallest gaps in my nostrils. I vomited into the space in front of me. I opened my eyes, unable to see anything as I was surrounded by an all-consuming darkness while I tried to get up. When I put my hand on the ground next to me I felt something warm and sticky. I immediately lifted my hand, not wanting to get any more of the gooey substance on my body than I already had. I didn't know what it was, but I realised that I was sitting in something just like it. My trousers soaking with the substance. I heard a sound from beside me and extended my arm in its general direction. I felt cold metal bars and used them to wipe off whatever was on my hand.
"Cole?"
It was Amelia.
"Where are we?"
The last thing I remembered was running toward that murdering monster, my mother. My heart hurt as I recollected reading the names:
Elon Gatner
Rebecca Kelser
Malcolm Myers

The Cost of Good Intentions

Etched into that terrible monument. I had become so obsessed with those stupid drawings, not ever thinking about anything else. How could I have been so blind? Why did I not question how it had become so easy to adapt to life here. I knew what kind of a person my mother was. She never once hid it from me when I was growing up, always only doing things for her own personal benefit, and now it was too late. My friends were dead, and it was all my fault. I didn't question her at all. Their blood was on my hands.

I began to cry. I thought that my life was bad in Nod; I thought that there couldn't be anything worse than going to Malcolm Myers Limited every day, but I had been wrong. I was trapped here, death surrounding me, with my only company being the woman whose best friend I had killed. It seemed fitting that I should end up here with her, as my own personal torture chamber for all the pain I had caused. My friends an added consequence of the results of my selfishness.

"I'm sorry," I sobbed, I was apologizing for all of it, because I didn't know what else to do. I knew it wouldn't make anything better, but it was the only thing that I felt was right.

"It's not your fault."

"Yes, it is, all of it is. Elon, Beck, Malcolm. it's all my fault and I'm sorry. I'm so fucking sorry. I didn't even try, I didn't even care anymore, it was like it made no difference whether they were around or not, they helped me through so much and they cared about me, even Malcolm is his own way. And Rory? I can't get his face out of my head now. He is everywhere I go, I didn't mean it, I swear, I was just trying to protect my friends and now they're gone, and I'm here, and I don't deserve to be."

"You can't believe that Cole. I know what it's like to feel guilty about being the one to survive. My mom died when she gave birth to me and I thought my dad was dead before I got here, I spent years feeling guilty, thinking I was being punished somehow, and maybe some part of me still feels that way now. It's so much worse knowing what my dad has become, and I can't help but feel that maybe it would be better if I never knew he was alive. I could have gone on pretending that he was a great man who died tragically, but instead I realize he is a monster and that is hard to accept, but I can't take blame for that as much as you can't take blame for the death of your friends."

A door creaked open, a single ray of light expanded as the door opened wider and wider.

I wished that they had just left it closed.

I would never get the image out of my head.

I could now see that the liquid on the floor was blood. It pooled around a pile of bodies that extended all the way to the top of my cage.

Amelia was in a cage next to me with a pile next to her that was just as high. Their white uniforms were now crimson red as each of their faces contorted, looking at me with an expression of eternal excruciating pain.

Amelia let out a blood curling scream as she observed the scene around her.

All feeling had left my body as I watched my mother walk into the room when the officer who had opened the door stepped aside.

The Cost of Good Intentions

Her clothes were spotless, as clean as you could ever possibly make them, but I knew how dirty her hands really were.

She paced around the room, her high heels sharply tapping the floor in a deadly precise rhythm. She looked to be deep in thought. My eyes glued to her as I wondered how many people someone had to kill before they became nose blind to the suffocating smell that filled the air in this room.

She cleared her throat before she began to speak in a measured tone.

"I have done everything I can to make your adjustment to life in Clayland as smooth as possible. It bre-"

"Like drugging your own fucking son?" Amelia screamed at my mother.

"Young lady, I tolerate you because of my love for my husband, the next time you interrupt me I will make sure to have his full support as I put a bullet in your head."

Amelia was silent, so my mother continued.

"I have given both of you more access to your deepest passions than would have ever been possible in your lives in Nod. I cured you of your addiction, son," she stopped pacing to look at me before continuing to walk and continued her speech, "and gave you the best roof you've ever had over your head, Amelia. You didn't pay to be here, and you don't have to work to earn your keep, your inclusion was one out of the goodness of my heart and this is how you repay me. By trying to attack me when you should be soundly asleep. It pains me to see my own son, and my stepdaughter take advantage of my good grace. The normal punishment for such a blatant crime would be death. But I am nothing if not merciful, and I would like to give you both the opportunity to think about what you have done and reconsider your feeling towards me. I hope that you take it."

She walked out the room, and the officer let the door close behind her as they left us to sit in the cages with the mountains of bodies.

We sat in silence for a while before Amelia spoke.

"Cole?"

"Yes?"

"I forgive you."

We spent weeks in those cages. The time dragged on, the only times we saw anything was when the door opened in the evenings for them to pile fresh bodies into the cages next to us, and when a servant would bring us each a glass of water as my mother asked if we were ready to embrace our lives in Clayland. Amelia took the lead in refusing every time, and I followed suit. I couldn't betray her I had just been cleared of all my guilt and couldn't bear the thought of doing something so unforgivable. Every day Amelia told me different stories about what she used to do with Rory. I listened to her describe their endless adventures, constantly moving around different parts of Nod, she told me of their inside jokes and Rory's support of her dream to write. She had written poems and left them all around different parts of Nod, under garbage bags, on random window ledges, even buried in the soil in parks. I couldn't fathom how someone who had experienced as much pain and suffering as the one who sat next to me could talk about their experience the way that she did.

The Cost of Good Intentions

I didn't have nearly as much to say, and as the days went on the conversations got shorter before we both eventually saved all the strength we had left. It was harder to stay awake and there was no clear end in sight.

I thought of my father.

He taught me to shoot when I was young. It was one of his preferred pastimes. He would go to different shooting ranges and try to hit all the targets. I wasn't really interested, but he kept on insisting that I join him, and after our third move I decided to give it a try. I had no friends, and I was in the mood for something to do. I went with him a few times after the first occasion, not because I liked it, but because I realized that I liked spending time with him. Especially at the beginning of the day when he was still sober. His love for shooting was so clear, and I paid such deep attention to everything he showed me. He taught me so much about the different types of rounds, he even knew how much each of them weighed.

But it didn't take long for him to stop shooting. His love for shooting never overcame his newfound dependence on alcohol. He couldn't hold the rifle steady, or shoot the targets, anymore. It was sad, really, watching a man fall out of love with the one thing that made living remotely bearable for him. He hated it after a while. Hated the fact that he no longer knew all the latest news about the guns available at the range. Hated the fact that his name was no longer a feature on the records board when he went to the shooting ranges. I think he mostly hated the fact that he was no longer in control, and he wasn't able to live on his own terms. The alcohol had taken away something much worse than his job. It had taken away his freedom. His freedom to decide what his top priority was, because it was no longer an option, it was drink or die. I promised myself that I wouldn't ever let it come to that, I wouldn't ever be a slave to substance. Yet I sat in that cage, and I had been just like him.

I was weak, my strength had all but left me when the door opened on one of the days and I opened my eyes to see Elliot being dragged into the room. I could see patches of blood on his dark skin as they opened the door to my cage and threw him in before leaving the room.

His body laid on top of my left foot.

I suppose he lived out his usefulness.

It went dark again before I heard Amelia start to move. I could hear her coming closer to me, stopping right by where the bars separated us.

"We need to get out of here, Cole."

I didn't know how she thought that was going to be possible. I was weak and didn't have any ideas.

"Do you want to take my mother's deal?" I whispered.

"No," an edge of defiance in her voice. "It will never come to that."

"What if it was that or death?" I think she picked up the hint of desperation that lingered in my question because she suddenly grabbed my hand and squeezed it.

"I haven't had much of anything in my life, but I've had more than most. Through all of my adversity, I held onto choice. My choice. The choice to not listen to what anything, inanimate or animate, tells me I am capable of doing. It is when you realise that on the other side of fear is freedom that you truly start to live out your potential. So, I won't allow you to sit there for one more second and pretend you are a victim. Whether you realize it or not, you still have the choice to change. The choice to be better, to do better. You still have something to offer. If you live one more second, I want you to make sure that in that second you are choosing to change. You are breaking your chains, and not allowing this world to claim you as an easy victim. I want you to promise me that you're going to claw and scratch and bite your way through this fight against injustice. Maybe you will be a victim but do your part in ensuring that you are the last one."

"I promise," I whispered.

"Good, now I think I have a plan."

CHAPTER 21

We were leaning against the wall when they brought the bodies in. The cage door opened, and the new bodies were dropped onto the floor in Amelia's cage and then into mine.

"Officer, I think he is dead, he hasn't moved for a while, you better let his mom know," Amelia said.

I felt the light from the officer's gun land on my face. It hovered there for a few seconds before I heard the officer enter the cage.

"Hey, you," the officer said to me.

I didn't move.

I felt his hand on my shoulder as he shook me. I let my head lull back and forth a couple of times until I saw the light move away from my eyes, and he took his hand off of my shoulder. I grabbed his hand and opened my eyes, startling him. I used all my energy as I hit his hand and he dropped the gun.

I punched him in the face a few times before I grabbed the gun and pointed it straight at his face.

He put his arms up as he remained crouched on one knee in front of me as I stood up. His nose was bloody and there was so much fear in his eyes.

"Give her the keys to her cell."

I watched as he moved his right hand slowly towards the set of keys dangling from his waist.

He unclipped them and threw them in Amelia's direction, she grabbed them and began opening the door to her cell.

I was surprised when I heard her say.

The Cost of Good Intentions

"Do it, Cole."

I realized that she wanted me to shoot him, and that was a step too far for me.

"Give me the keys," I didn't move the gun from his head.

Amelia handed me the keys in my free hand. I watched the officers terrified eyes follow me as I kept the gun on his head while I moved around him before exiting the cell and locking him in.

"Do you know how many people he's killed? He DESERVES it," she was furious.

"That's not for us to decide, Amelia. If we killed him, how are we any different?"

"They're just going to let him out again, and he'll carry on doing it."

"I won't, I swear," the officer's voice was trembling when he said it.

"Of- course you would say that now," Amelia said to him.

"Please, I won't hurt you I swear! If they find me in here and you're gone they'll just kill my family and replace me with someone else."

"What do you mean somebody else?" Amelia asked, "Everyone else is dead."

"No, they're not, they're still in Nod, please, I'm telling the truth."

I looked at Amelia. Her cheekbones were sharper, her skin was pale. The effects of our starvation on full display. I was sure I didn't look much better.

"How do we get back?" she asked, "How do we get back to Nod?"

The Cost of Good Intentions

"There's an elevator down the corridor, I can show you, you'll need my code."

I trusted him, but Amelia seemed hesitant.

"We don't have many other options," I whispered.

"Okay, but if anything seems off you need to shoot him, Cole."

I nodded and opened the cage.

I stepped back, aiming the gun at the officer as he kept his hands up and walked through the door.

We followed him and I realized that we were in the servants' quarters.

They did this intentionally, to make sure the servants knew. They kept these bodies here as a reminder of what happens when you don't follow the rules in this fucked up place.

I saw the elevator at the end of the corridor, opposite another door that was different to every door in Clayland. This door was wooden and had our parent's names in thick steel letters.

My heart raced as we approached. I kept thinking they were going to open the door and stop us.

The officer reached a keypad and started typing in the code.

"What's the code?" Amelia asked.

"I can't tell you that."

Even now, with a gun pointed at him, there was some form of loyalty. As if telling us that code was as good as giving us the secret to the universe. I had been blind, up until this point but now it was so hard to ignore the stupidity of the officer. He was standing in the way of people trying to fix his biggest problem by bringing an end to Clayland. All because he thought that if he gave up that code, he gave up his usefulness, and we would end his life.

I lowered the gun.

He stared at me and looked me in the eye as he told us the code and stepped aside as Amelia entered it and the doors opened.

Amelia and I got into the elevator and the officer tried to follow. She stopped him on the threshold of the door.

"What do you think you're doing?" She asked him.

"I can't do this anymore; I know some people who can help you. I need to just get my family, make sure they're safe, and then we can take this place down. If people know the truth, they won't be able to get anyone to come here."

Amelia let him in.

He stood in the middle of us, and the doors started to close.

They were halfway closed when the door opposite the elevator opened. The door to our parent's room. I watched as my mother walked out in pyjamas, with a scowl on her face as she lifted a gun and shot the officer in the face.

The doors closed fully, and we began to rise.

Amelia searched the officer's body, and she took car keys from his pocket. we both cried as she did it, but it didn't stop her from doing it anyway. In the last year I had witnessed more death than all the 26 years before. The first time I just stood still because I was in shock, and I didn't know what else to do. In that elevator I cried because I was numb. I thought of all the people who were slaughtered, and I cried for all of them at once. I cried because I was no longer shocked that this is what people were capable of. It was different when you watched it on the news, because you weren't there, you didn't feel like you were so involved in it, but the truth was that we were. That thought alone would have pushed me over the edge, into a guilt so strong that I might have never gotten out, but Amelia had changed me in the cage. I understood my part in this, but all the needless death couldn't be for nothing. I couldn't change what had happened, nothing was going to bring that officer back, but I could try to make sure that something like that doesn't happen again.

The elevator doors opened, and we stepped out to what I immediately identified as Elon's back yard. I looked behind me as the elevator sank into the ground and became a part of the grass.

We needed to run; they would be after us.

I was so weak as I led Amelia to the officer's marked Police car. I climbed behind the wheel, Amelia got into the passenger seat. We couldn't go to my apartment, it would be the first place they looked. I was so hungry I could feel how much energy I had used just to get to that car.

We didn't have time to think, they wouldn't be far behind. I put the car in first and drove, to nowhere in particular. When I felt like we were far enough I slowed down and for the first time since we escaped I was able to look at the houses. There were no more lights on. We were in one of the richer parts of Nod, I thought it would be the safest considering most of the rich were down in Clayland. All the cars on the street were parked outside but it was a ghost town.

I pulled over at one of the houses, unable to go any further. We got out the car and walked to the door.

The Cost of Good Intentions

I tried the handle, and it gave way. The door groaned as I opened it and stepped into the house. We took quick glances in every room until we found the kitchen. The cupboards were overflowing with food. Amelia and I each grabbed a tin of green beans, and she started opening all the drawers in the house. She found a tin opener and opened her tin before devouring its contents and handing the tin opener to me. When I finished eating I reached up to get another.

"No," she grabbed my wrist.

"Why not?"

"It won't make you feel any better, we've not eaten in too long."

I felt sorry for her, I knew she was speaking from experience.

She didn't let me linger on the thought.

"I had an idea while you were driving," she said. "We need to go back to your old work."

"What? Why?"

"Malcolm had information on his phone that explained all of this. If we can get that information we can distribute it, that officer said that if people know the truth, they wouldn't go to Clayland. That's how we stop them, Cole."

It sounded like a terrible plan, filled with too much hope and not enough reality, but it was the only one we had. What chance did we have when we were still trying to make sense of everything ourselves? We needed that information.

I thought of taking some supplies, but every time I tried to do so in the past, they either got stolen or damaged, so I decided against it, instead I grabbed one more tin of green beans and the tin opener to keep in the car.

We were leaving the house and as we were walking, I took notice of how clean everything seemed to be. It was strange. The people who lived here obviously knew about the plan to move to Clayland, but why would someone clean their house so thoroughly if they never planned on coming back? And how was it so clean after all these months? Why was there so much food in the cupboard? I listened carefully, and besides the sound of our footsteps I couldn't hear anything. We were definitely alone. I couldn't make sense of it.

We got to the car and I drove towards Malcolm Myers Limited. When we arrived, we got out the car and started walking towards the tall glass building. Amelia looked up at the building before we walked through the doors. We jumped over the turnstiles and I entered the code to the stairwell. I was out of breath when we got to the top. I opened the doors and watched Amelia as she walked in and observed everything in the room. Her head moved from left to right as she took in every little detail.

I stood looking at her before I realized that she wasn't in awe of it. She was in shock as she had discovered that our only plan was, most likely, a dead end. All the computers were smashed, the pieces of broken telephones were scattered everywhere as they lay next to flipped desks.

She was silent, she stared at the ground for a while before she looked at me.

She was about to speak when we heard a noise come from Malcolm's office. We both crouched down as we heard the door handle turn.

The Cost of Good Intentions

"Cole!?"

It couldn't be.

"Cole!?" It came out more like a sob.

I knew the voice.

I stood up.

Tears filled my eyes as I looked at Elon.

CHAPTER 22

That moment encapsulated all of the confusion I had felt for the last few months. I observed every inch of him, and after all this time nothing had changed. I had suddenly become all too aware of how my ribs were more present and my fingers more bony. I couldn't help but question the guilt I felt because in that moment I wanted to find him starved and desolate if anything at all.

The past few months had shed a new light on our relationship. A light that differed from the usual radiance I once felt when I was in Elon's company. It was true that when I stood looking at his name on that terrible monument, I had felt melancholic at the loss of my best friend. Looking into Elon's dark blue eyes at that moment was like looking into the eyes of a stranger.

A moment passed with neither of us moving before I broke the silence by asking the only question that I felt was worth asking.

"What the fuck?"

And just like the moment where I found out about Beck, he knew that I knew what he had done. He knew that I knew he was the creator of Clayland.

His eyes dropped; he was unable to look at me. A few tears dropped from his face to the tiled floor.

"I'm sorry, I tried to stop it, Cole. I really did."

"You shouldn't have tried to start it in the first place," I couldn't hide my hurt.

"I know, Cole. I was scared, okay?" he looked up at me, his tears were in full flow.

The Cost of Good Intentions

"Scared? What could you possibly have to be scared of?"

"The planet was dying, Cole. I didn't know what else to do."

"So, you just decided to build some underground world and let everyone on the surface kill each other?"

He looked away again.

"Cole," Amelia whispered.

"And how ironic that you somehow manage to survive this without any indication that you've suffered," I continued.

"Cole," Amelia whispered again.

"Do you know that they killed Beck, and Malcolm!?" my voice was rising, I couldn't control it. My anger had flared, and he still couldn't look at me. "LOOK AT ME!" I screamed.

"Cole," Amelia had said even softer.

"What!?" I screamed at her.

It was only then that I looked at Amelia. She looked stiff. She looked like she had seen a ghost. I calmed down when I looked at her. Why was she staring at him like that? Why did she look so pale?

"The people didn't kill each other, Cole," she was still staring at him. Out of the corner of my eye I noticed that Elon had twitched when she said it.

"The cops killed the people on the surface, Cole."

My head was spinning as I processed what she had said. It couldn't be true. This was too much. My heart hurt as I went over everything in my head and realized that she was right, but I needed to be sure.

"Elon?" my voice broke as I said his name.

"It's true."

The Cost of Good Intentions

I'd never been shot before. Never been stabbed. The worst wound I ever had was when I had fallen off my bicycle when I was learning how to ride. I thought that was the worst pain in the world, that I had felt the worst that the world has to offer. The wound scabbed over and was healed in less than a month. When I looked at Elon now. A man I had trusted with every fibre of my being. A man I had supported without question through every stage of our lives. I knew that this wound would take a long time to heal, if it ever did, because this wasn't like a wound you get when you fall off your bike. When you get one of those you know what went wrong: you lost balance, or you rode over something. When you have an emotional wound, you start to question every element of every relationship you've ever had. You start to question everything about yourself and every time you question you get further away from the answer. You think, "Well I was really wrong about that, what else have I been wrong about?" and that kind of doubt can lead to all kinds of ugly places.

"How did any of this happen? Where is the sun? Please just help me understand," There was no emotion in my voice, I felt numb.

Elon took a deep breath and wiped the tears from his cheeks.

"The sun is still in the sky it's just covered by a projection. There were too many people, Cole. The pollution was too much so we had to do something. I started building Elex a few years back when I first got told that we had about 10 years to save the planet."

"Elex?" Amelia asked.

The Cost of Good Intentions

"The underground city in my backyard. I got some scientists to work on making a projection strong enough to block out the sun, to use as a signal, and sent out information on what would be required to be a citizen."
"You mean money?" I said with an extra sting in my voice.
"No, not just money. I wanted it to be equal opportunity. I offered cheaper packages, and even packages for people to work for a place in Elex," he looked like he was proud of this, like he honestly thought that it was a mercy from him that anyone who couldn't pay be given a chance to live.
"I even offered for their families to be able to stay for free while only one member works. But the closer it came to the time the more guilt I felt for what had to be done for Earth to heal. So, I tried to stop it. I spiked your drinks that night at my house and activated the lounge security, knowing that you would know the code, and I came here. I had an override to stop the messages that have told people to stay inside every day for months now, but somehow they knew. They knew I was too soft hearted to go through with it. They sent people to kill me at my house, and when I got here, to the office, I found all the computers smashed to pieces and another person trying to kill me. That's when I called you, Cole. I managed to pay the guy they sent after me to tell your mother, who he said was the new leader of Elex, that I was dead, so they would stop looking for me, and I have been able to stay under their radar since, only leaving here to get food and water."
Amelia walked to Elon, never once looking away from him, and punched him across the jaw. She shook her hand and Elon held his jaw.
"Why would you do that? Who is this, Cole?"

The Cost of Good Intentions

"You don't know me?"

"No! Why would I?"

"Well then how can you decide my fate?"

Elon was silent.

"The first time I ever heard about your little project I was inside its ugly walls. I never got a choice to be there, and I want to tell you, Elon Gatner, if I did, I wouldn't have gone."

"Co-"

"Shut up! How is it possible for you, who probably has the biggest carbon footprint in this room, to say that someone who can't afford to eat needs to die to save the world that you destroyed?"

Amelia was seething.

"I lost my best friend on the day that your stupid fucking plan started, because everyone was scared and confused. At one point I felt like maybe I would have been better off dying with Rory in the street. But his death won't be in vain. I will go to the ends of this planet to make sure that you and all your friends look in the eyes of all the families who are now fractured because you decided to play God and tell them why you did it. I want to see if they think you are so merciful when your twisted words get untangled and read loudly and clearly, 'I have decided that I am worth more than you'."

"So, was I supposed to let everyone die, because you want to feel like you're important?" Elon scowled; his true colours were coming to light.

"No! You were supposed to at least give us a fucking choice!"

"It would never work; you're living in a delusional fantasy. Whenever you give people the power to choose, they choose wrong."

"And you choose right?" she asked sarcastically.

"More often than not."

"So, I suppose you standing here, having almost been killed was all part of the plan then?"

Elon went silent again.

"Tell me, was Cole ever going to be allowed into Elex?"

"Yes! I paid for him and Beck, I would never leave them behind," Elon smiled at me, and a little bit of the warmness between us came back before Amelia destroyed it again. She looked at me and realized that I appreciated that Elon had done that.

"Don't fucking fall for it, Cole! You can't give him a pass just because he's your friend, that's how it starts," she turned back to Elon, "You make me sick."

"For trying to help my friends?"

"For making sure that you don't have to sacrifice a thing while everyone else has their lives turned upside down."

She was right. It was so hard being there, looking at him, and for the first time truly understanding the extent of his selfishness.

I didn't have long to dwell on my emotion because I heard the door from the stairwell being opened and a gun being cocked.

"Get down!" I shouted. Everyone jumped to the ground and hid behind the closest desks to them before six rounds were fired into the space where we were standing.

I heard the gun being reloaded before someone shouted.

The Cost of Good Intentions

"Come out, pigs!" they must have seen the car outside and assumed we were cops.

"We're not the police," I shouted without lifting my head.

"Nice try!"

"He's telling the truth!" Amelia shouted.

Elon was still silent.

"I'm going to raise my hands and slowly stand so we can talk," I said, trying to stay calm.

When I did it, I found myself staring down the barrel of his gun. He took one look at me, taking in the severity of my malnutrition and knew that I was telling the truth.

"There are three of us," I said as he lowered the gun. I noticed all the scars and burn marks. They were all over, covering the entirety of his dark muscular arms.

"Everyone stand up."

Amelia stood immediately and walked over to grab Elon and pull him up as he showed no signs of doing so on his own.

"I'm Cole, that's Amelia and Elon," I said as I gestured to each of them in turn.

"I'm Jacob," the man said as he turned to start walking to the door. "There's a group of us, the others are on the floors below, I need to warn them, we are more shoot first and ask questions later, especially when it comes to pigs."

"A group?" I started to feel a little bit of hope as I followed him, "How many?"

"20 of us in the building," he put his hand out to stop me at the door before he shouted down the stairwell, "We've got 3 casuals up here, no pigs," Jacob turned to me, "You can go now, they won't shoot, let's get back to safety and then we can talk."

I nodded, "Let's go," I said to Amelia and Elon.

We walked down the stairwell, Jacob was following us, on all the different levels there were people with guns outside the doors. They were all in dirty casual clothing and were expressionless as we walked past them and down the stairs. When we got to the ground floor, we followed a guard out the door. Jacob took the lead, he seemed to be looking everywhere at once as we walked through a few streets in the suburban area that surrounded Malcolm Myers Limited. We seemed to have reached our destination when we stood outside of an ordinary yellow house, we walked up the stairs, each one groaning from our weight and walked through the wooden front door that had been painted white. The number 77 was on the door. When we entered the house everything looked normal. Jacob led us into, what looked like, a child's bedroom. The floors were wooden and there was a rug with a cartoon character in the centre of the room. I watched as Jacob lifted the rug. Everything looked normal apart from a gap that was just big enough to fit a hand into. I watched Jacob slide his hand into the gap and retrieve a key before he stood and put the rug back in place. He walked toward a bookshelf that I hadn't noticed, and he took one of the books out before he inserted the key he had retrieved into the newly created gap. I heard a click before he pulled the bookshelf towards himself and revealed an elevator.

He put a code into a keypad that was next to the elevator and the doors opened as he stepped aside and motioned for us to enter.

The Cost of Good Intentions

We didn't have any other plan so the three of us obliged. Elon and Amelia were inside the elevator when Jacob stopped me.

"Give them this when you get down there," he handed me a token with a fist on it, "I need to go carry on with the searches."

I looked him in the eye and nodded before I stepped into the elevator.

I watched the doors close, Jacob stared at all of us as they did. I wasn't sure if we were making the right choice but what other option did we have?

The elevator began to descend.

"We're really going to just trust this guy?" Elon asked in a flabbergasted manner.

"You're going to question whether we should trust someone?" Amelia scoffed.

"I'm just saying, we just did what he wanted without really questioning him, once. I mean, he did tell Cole we could talk when we were safe and now he's left us."

"It's alm-" Amelia began another attack on Elon's questionable morals before I interrupted.

"He's got a point, Amelia, maybe we should have questioned him a bit more."

She looked annoyed as the elevator doors opened to reveal at least 15 rifles aimed directly at us.

CHAPTER 23

I saw red dots shifting from side-to-side as they waited patiently for their wielders to pull the trigger. The dots danced across our torsos as we looked into the eyes of the men and woman ready to take our lives. I remembered the token.

"I…I have a token," I stuttered, surprised at how dry my throat suddenly felt.

I watched as the men with the guns moved to create a gap in the middle where a woman walked through. She was fierce. Her stare could do more damage than any of the guns that surrounded her. Her arms were taut with muscle, each sinew holding the next in a tightly woven unit that looked impermeable.

"Bring it to me."

Nobody moved.

"Bring me the token."

I realized that she was talking to me, so I started walking to her. Some of the guns followed me but I was too focused on her stare. It was hypnotizing. I handed her the token without breaking eye contact.

She looked down at it. A hint of a smile on her lips.

"How did you get here?" her voice was full of force, the kind that demanded authority.

"Jacob brought us," I said, my voice still coming out unevenly.

"Ahhh, Jacob, a true warrior," her smile grew as I watched the recollection of a memory linger in her golden eyes, "Lower them," she said softly, and I watched all the guns that had been pointed at us drop to the sides of their owners.

"What is your name?"

"Cole."

There was a flicker of something in her face.

"And your friends?"

"Amelia and Spencer," I said, looking away from her eyes when I lied. If she had noticed she didn't say anything. The first time she looked away from me was when Elon tried to correct me before Amelia kicked his leg to shut him up.

"Walk with me, the three of you," the woman said as she turned and began walking, not waiting to see if we were following her or not.

The three of us walked behind her and looked at our surroundings. We seemed to be inside a cave, with battery operated spotlights surrounding the perimeter of the area. I looked around and saw hundreds of people sitting around campfires, their tired faces being illuminated by the flames. We walked towards a tent that was pitched at the back of the cave, the only tent in the vicinity.

The tent was a small one, only big enough to fit a small table that held a candle alongside a notebook, and a stretcher that acted as a bed.

"My name is Athena, I am the leader of The Rejected, a group formed to combat the slaughter aimed toward the poor of society. A slaughter which began the day that the sun disappeared from the sky and continues to this day in the latest development of the Class Wars, a war that has been silently waged for decades," Athena began to say.

"We know about the slaughter," Amelia interrupted.

"No doubt you do, Amelia Clark," Athena said with a suspicious undertone in her voice.

"How do you know my name?" Amelia struggled to hide her shock. I watched as her muscles tensed while I struggled to keep myself calm.

"I know many things. I know you're the daughter of Ben Clark, husband and second in command to Eleanor Clay, the mother of Cole Clay," Athena's gaze turned to me as she paused, silence filled every inch of the tent. The voices from outside faded away as I held my breath and wondered what Athena had planned for us.

"Tell me, what business do the children of two tyrants have with someone I've never heard of?" she glanced at Elon before fixing her stare on me once more.

"He's a friend of mine," I said, finding it easier to tell a half truth than a full lie.

"And since when do the rich care about friends?"

"We are not like our parents," Amelia said. "We left Clayland the moment we had an opportunity because we knew it was wrong."

"Was that before or after you sat around for months doing nothing while innocent men and woman got slaughtered inside and outside of *Clayland*. In his last communications Elliot told me that the two of you had been actively using the art facility there for months without any real attempts to stop the slaughter you, Amelia Clark, witnessed in the dark. I can't get hold of Elliot anymore; anyone care to explain?"

My eyes dropped to the ground.

"I see. That is…unfortunate, he was a good man."

"We are not your enemies," Amelia said sternly.

The Cost of Good Intentions

"It just seems strange that the two children of the leaders of my enemies are found with someone I've not heard of a few weeks after communication with my internal source goes dark, doesn't it?"

I saw a look in Amelia's eyes and knew she was contemplating telling Athena who Elon was and what we were trying to do. I couldn't risk it, I didn't know how Athena would react to that kind of information, and I didn't want to find out. I didn't have to intervene because Athena continued.

"It is a matter we can discuss later. With you being the only two who have knowledge of Clayland, and being the children of the leaders there, it pains me to say that you are necessary at this moment."

I felt a slight sense of relief, before Athena continued with a more threatening tone.

"However, the moment I deem you to be unnecessary you will have to answer for all the lives that have been lost due to your inactivity. For the time being, go get something to eat and get some rest. You are dismissed."

We turned to walk away I could see Amelia was furious. I gave her a look to let her know that whatever she wanted to say was not worth it. We were here now, and we were still alive somehow, we needed to make the most of it.

We walked out of the tent and had a look around. We saw a huge stack of tins in a corner of the cave so the three of us headed towards it to get some food.

There was no free space anywhere, where we could have a private conversation. So, we took our food and went to sit around one of the many campfires in the cave.

The Cost of Good Intentions

Everyone around the fire was silent, each one staring into the flames as if they would hold the answers to the internal questions they had. Their clothes were well worn, and their faces were filthy. Every person had a gun next to them. We ate our food in silence, feeding into the moment of reflection.

I thought about all that Athena had said. I felt guilty because she had been right, what had we done to try and help? I had accepted my new-found privilege with open arms, not once did I question anything around me. If Amelia hadn't told me to stop drinking the juice I would still be there. I thought about what I would do if I could do it over with the knowledge I had then. What could we have possibly done to stop our parents from murdering innocent people for their own personal gain?

The questions kept flooding my brain before I decided I had had enough. My body felt tired, and weak, like I hadn't slept for days. So, I laid down on the hard floor and stared up at the roof of the cave before I closed my eyes and fell asleep.

CHAPTER 24

AMELIA

How dare she? She had no right to question us after all that we had done. This ignorant woman stood in front of us and judged us without knowing anything about what we had been through, and Cole just accepted it. I looked at his sharp cheekbones and his clothes that had become too big for him and watched as he sank into a state of self-loathing as Athena questioned our integrity. She praised Elliot, the man who had actively contributed to life in Clayland, and scrutinized us, the ones who had actively tried to dismantle Clayland from the moment we discovered all the wrongdoings occurring in its walls.

I looked around at all the people in the cave, everyone was silent, with the same expression of the people sitting in the hospital waiting room when I was 9 years old. I wondered how many of them had lost someone in the past few months. I wondered if Athena had questioned them like she did us, or was it only because she assumed we were working against her somehow that we were interrogated so aggressively?

Another trait of the Before Times. The system corrupting something as pure as trust to make it impossible to determine whether a stranger's motives were as pure as they said, immediately forcing anyone in any situation to assume the worst rather than the best. It was how they had divided us, by making us fight amongst ourselves instead of focusing on the real problem, and Athena was making that mistake. She was so blinded by her hurt and anger that she couldn't see she had her three most valuable assets right in front of her.

Cole had fallen asleep next to me, and Elon next to him. I looked at the two of them, the difference was enormous. I first wondered how Cole hadn't been able to see through Elon, how he hadn't been able to know that Elon only cared about himself. I saw it the moment when Cole told him about the death of their friend, Beck, and Elon's reaction to the news was to defend himself rather than take responsibility for the part he played in it. I stopped wondering about Cole's ignorance when I thought about my dad and realized that I had been exactly the same.

I watched as Cole's chest gently rose before falling again, noticing how peaceful he looked. In the cage he told me about his personal war with addiction, fuelled by fear. Fear of being inadequate, fear of being homeless, fear of the judgement of strangers. It was a vicious cycle that was only enhanced through the contents of a bottle, a self-inflicted sadness that he had been conned into deeming necessary.

Him breaking that cycle might have been the only positive thing to come from those past few months, and what a positive it was. I hadn't known Cole Clay very long, but I could see the shift. I could see the clarity in his thought. I saw him reward himself when he thought nobody else was looking. He would give off a little smile in recognition of the fact that he was able to finally do something that felt like it was of his own accord. This Class War had given him something back that he never knew he had lost in the first place. I could see the hunger in him to end every last trace of the system that had brought him to his knees without him knowing it. The world needed more Cole

The Cost of Good Intentions

Clays. It needed heroes who acknowledged their wrongdoing and fought tooth and nail to make it right.

After a while of sitting in front of the fire, surrounded by all the survivors, we were once again summoned to Athena's tent. She had tied her dark brown hair up, adding a unique femininity to her otherwise brutish look.
"I have decided what your best use is," Athena began before I interrupted her.
"How refreshing," I said sarcastically.
"Sarcasm is the lowest form of wit, Ms Clark," Athena replied. I saw Elon and Cole glance at each other, both trying not to smile. I ignored them and shifted my attention back to Athena as she continued.
"A few men will escort you back to Clayland, where you will be used to barter the release of the servants."
"It won't work," Cole said, looking deadly serious. "They don't care about us, they'll kill us if they get the chance."
"Well, it is our only option, and is a risk I am willing to take," Athena said calmly.
"So, we should just be led to our probable slaughter because you haven't been able to come up with a better plan in a couple of hours?" I was struggling to keep the shock out of my voice.
"Each moment that passes is a moment where another servant might die. I am not afforded the luxury of time, and if you really want to know I will gladly share that this was not a difficult decision to make as you all have had a role to play in the deaths of all servants up until this point. So, it is a win in both regards, as if you are successful you will have been able to repay your debt and rot amongst

your true brethren, and if you are unsuccessful you would have paid for all the pain you have caused to every family out there due to your inexcusable inaction."

I could see Cole was buying it. I watched him look at the floor and contemplate all that Athena had said. I saw Elon start to panic as he realized that Eleanor would kill him if she was given half the chance.

I couldn't stand it one moment longer.

"You're no better than them," I said to Athena.

"Excuse me?"

"You heard me," I said, my voice rising.

"You sit here in your tent and order others around like we are nothing. Once again, we are stuck somewhere without much of a say in anything as you take it upon yourself to make a decision regarding our lives. You talk about our inaction? Where were you when all the servants were getting slaughtered? Where were you when we starved in a cage and watched the bodies get thrown in every day?"

"Ms Clark," Athena warned.

"No! We are not your pawns that you get to play with in your stupid fucking war."

"We are all involved whether we want to be or not! Now get out of my sight before I change my mind and put a bullet in you myself."

A man with a gun held open the door to the tent and gestured for us to leave.

I gave her one last glare before leaving and following a man to the elevator. Everyone in the cave was looking at us as we walked towards the open doors of the elevator and stepped inside. My rage silently hummed in my chest as I thought about the fact that we were being sent to our probable deaths due to our, 'inaction' while a cave full of people sat and did nothing.

The door closed and we began our ascent to the surface.

"She's going to kill me," were the first words Elon had spoken since we had first entered the cave.

"She's going to kill all of us," I said, unable to think of anything comforting to say.

"We deserve it," Cole said, still feeling guilty about Athena's false claims.

"No, we don't deserve it, Cole."

"If we had done something sooner maybe we could have saved some of them."

"Done what, Cole?"

"I don't know, but something," he said blandly.

"Nothing we could have done would have changed anything, we would have just been another statistic, we needed more people, I just thought we had finally found them, but I was wrong."

The doors opened and we were greeted by Jacob who was sitting on the bed with his gun next to him.

He gave us a sad smile.

We left the house and walked to a black SUV that was parked across the street. Jacob opened the door to the back seat, and we all climbed in before he climbed into the driver seat and greeted a man who had been sitting in the car. We drove down the street with the headlights off. Another SUV trailed us as we were driven to Elon's house. We reached the street, it all looked so calm.

The Cost of Good Intentions

We got out of the car. Jacob and the man climbed out of the car we had travelled in, and another 5 men got out of the SUV that had followed us here.

We walked towards the secret elevator and stopped. I looked around and realized that all the guards were looking at us. They were expecting us to put in the code.

Why did they assume we knew the code?

None of us moved, unsure of what to do.

"Put in the code," Jacob said as he rested his hand on the gun that was tucked into his waistband.

"We don't know it," Cole said unconvincingly.

"Don't test our patience," said one of the other men.

I sighed as I crouched down and entered the code into the keypad. As I keyed in the last digit the elevator hissed as it rose from the ground and the doors opened.

I watched as four of the men walked in and told us to get into the elevator. The other three cramming in behind us when we entered. The elevator just managed to fit us all in as the doors closed and we descended.

Something wasn't right, but I couldn't quite figure it out before the doors opened and the three men in front of us aimed their guns in front of them, directly into the guns of Eleanor and my father.

"We have your children," said Jacob, calmly. "We want to talk."

"We don't negotiate with terrorists," Eleonor said, idiotically.

"Well, you do if you want your children to live," all the guards stopped pointing their guns at Eleanor and my father and pointed them at me and Cole.

The Cost of Good Intentions

I watched Eleanor and my father's eyes widen. They weren't looking at us, they were looking at Elon.

He was now smiling as I looked down to see the moment before he pulled the trigger of the gun he had in his left hand. I watched as Eleanor's face was filled with agony and terror.

My dad dropped his gun and put his hands up, while Eleanor dropped to the floor, clutching the bullet wound in her stomach as she was unable to stop blood from spilling through the gaps in her fingers.

"No!" Cole screamed.

I watched as he burst forward, breaking through the wall of men that surrounded us, and ran to his mother. It was heart breaking to witness Cole cradle his mother, a woman who had done nothing but manipulate and use her son, as he whispered a single word.

"Mom."

A glance shared between the two of them connected them in more ways than words ever could as her look apologized for all the pain she had caused her son. I watched the horror flood Cole's face as he saw his mother's eyes turn glassy and felt her body go limp.

His crying was hysterical and all we could do was watch as a son grieved for his mother.

"What have you done?" he wailed.

The smile had left Elon's face as he was now filled with a look of confusion.

My father stood with his hands up, not even shedding a tear at the passing of his wife.

Cole stood up and walked to Elon, taking his turn to punch Elon.

The Cost of Good Intentions

Elon held his jaw as he stepped out of the elevator, moving into the corridor of the servant's quarters and pulling a face as he smelled the pungent stench of the bodies for the first time.

"She was a monster, Cole," Elon said, still clutching his jaw.

"She was my mom! You're a monster!" Cole screeched.

I watched his eyes fill with sadness as he decided what to do next.

"Take them to their rooms," Elon said to Jacob. "Throw him in the cage," he said to another one of the men that had escorted us, while he looked at my father.

Jacob grabbed my arm and Cole's arm. Both of us struggled before more of the men grabbed us. I kicked and screamed as I was carried out of the servant's quarters and taken towards the corridor that led to the room I had stayed in before. A few of the servants pressed their faces against the glass windows on their doors. The hopelessness in that corridor was palpable.

I was thrown into the room and the door was closed. I heard a click as they locked the door so I wouldn't be able to go anywhere.

I sat and cried on the floor. We had been such fools. I cried as I realized we were back to square one, with no hope in sight.

The light went out, leaving me to sit with my sorrow in darkness as I wondered what I would do next.

CHAPTER 25

The lights came on, blinding me as I watched a smiling woman walk into the room with breakfast. Her smile sickened me. She placed the breakfast onto the table. The moment she set it down I smacked the tray off the table, spilling its contents onto the floor. She didn't break stride as she began to pick it up.

"I'll get you a fresh breakfast Ms Clark," she said, still smiling.

What was wrong with these people? How could they just go on like this, like this was any kind of a life worth living?

"When you've eaten, I'm required to escort you to the basketball court so that President Gatner can address all the residents of Elex."

I didn't speak, because I knew that if I opened my mouth I wouldn't be able to hold back all that I felt. I needed to save my rage for him. I was ready for war.

I didn't eat the food when the servant brought the fresh breakfast into my room, placing it on my table. I didn't even look at her. I looked in the mirror, into my own eyes. Before the day that the sun was gone I had spent years following Rory's instruction, he had more experience with homelessness, and knew more about how to get by on a day-to-day basis. I listened to him and followed him with whatever plan he had come up with. It was only in his absence that I had to become a leader in my own life. When that shift happened, I started to see what Rory was talking about. All these people were only here because they had something to gain from it. They only cared about

The Cost of Good Intentions

themselves. Their own safety or comfort. From the top to the bottom everyone in this place chose to leave Nod behind, knowing that everyone else would die. What excuse is good enough to do something like that?

I was bitter, and not just towards the top anymore. My bitterness spread throughout my body to the point where I couldn't find a good enough reason to greet the servant, because she was here by choice.

So, when she knocked on the door to take me to the basketball court, I didn't even acknowledge her as I walked past. I didn't slow down as she ran past me to lead me to the court when I already knew the way. I didn't thank her when she held the door open and ushered me inside to a room full of people. I just walked in and observed the thousands of guilty people that sat and waited for their new president's speech.

I watched as they laughed and smiled, and I hated all of it.

I saw Cole sitting at the top of the bleachers, not interacting with anyone.

He looked angry. His features softened when he saw me. His eyes asking me to sit with him.

There was a pull in my gut as I thought about what he must be feeling. My dad may be in a cage, but Cole's mom was gone, and that would take its toll on anyone.

I pushed and squeezed my way through people, not saying anything as I did. A few of them scowled at me as I went by, I didn't pay them any attention. When I reached the top of the bleachers I was surprised when Cole pulled me into a hug.

He didn't say anything, he just squeezed me.

"I'm sorry about your mom," I whispered.

The Cost of Good Intentions

"This ends today," he said, determinedly. I didn't have a chance to ask him what he meant before he let go of me as Elon walked into the room to a chorus of cheers. He casually strolled and waved as he made his way towards a podium with a microphone set up in the middle of the court.

I almost jumped out of my seat when I saw Athena follow him into the room with an entourage of armed men who dispersed to different sections of the court, but Cole stopped me.

The servants sat in their own section of the bleachers. They made up a tiny fraction of the people that were in the room.

Elon stopped at the podium, gripping the microphone and clearing his throat into it before the whole room went so silent that you could hear the breath of everyone present.

"Thank you all for coming on such short notice," he began.

Like we had a choice.

"I'd like to start by introducing the new Vice President of Elex, Athena Qayin," he paused as there was another chorus of cheers.

"Now I know times have been hard around here," he continued when the cheers began to subside, "But that ends now! Here, in Elex, we treat each other with dignity and respect. We are all equal, even though we all have different roles to play. I was informed, during my forced exile by the hands of the traitors Eleanor Clay and Ben Clark, that servants have had to share their living space with their families. It is unacceptable to expect the hard workers who make life in Elex possible to not be given something as simple as privacy when they are not busy selflessly seeing to our needs. I am a man of action rather than speech, and being such I want to make my first pledge as your leader and president. Each and every person, whether servant or guest will be entitled to their own rooms."

The crowd erupted. Elon smiled as he looked around the room, purposefully avoiding looking at me and Cole.

It was disgusting. I wondered how long Elon Gatner had planned this. The only people who didn't cheer whenever he paused were the servants and Cole and me. It was hard at that time to have any faith in humanity, because we sat in a room where majority of the people had been complicit in the murders of the servant's families, and yet they cheered like their favourite sports team had just won a trophy. Whether they had pulled the trigger or not they were all equally guilty. I had spent my entire life in the company of a few people, good people, and I had assumed that everyone else would be the same, but the reality was this: People were greedy, they only cared about the things that affected them and tried to ensure that everything was affecting them positively. They didn't care about the injustice that was right in front of them.

When everyone had stopped cheering and sat down, that was when Cole stood up.

He started to clap slowly as he walked down the bleachers towards the court. His claps echoed; people moved out of his way as he stared straight at Elon. He did a few sarcastic cheers, cupping his hands around his mouth as he did it, the room was completely silent as every eye was fixed on him.

The Cost of Good Intentions

"What a hero! You have saved us all!" he began, "How will we ever repay you?"

Elon smiled, nervously, a bead of sweat began to form on his forehead.

"Everyone gets a room! How did you ever manage that?" he feigned shock. "Wait, don't tell me! Can I have a guess?"

"Cole," Elon warned, standing a bit too close to the microphone as his warning was heard all over the room.

"Is it because the servant's families are lying dead in a cage just down the corridor?"

The room was silent as I watched a few guards raise their guns. Cole looked straight at them.

"Fucking shoot me, like you did the rest of them."

Athena looked at the guards and they lowered their weapons.

"How many people have to die before something changes?" Cole looked around the room as he said it, before he fixed his eyes on the servants.

"I used to be just like you, always following orders, getting told what was good for me and what wasn't. I was too scared to do something because I was taught to fear the consequences of not doing it. I was too invested to see that if enough of us just stopped doing what they wanted then their whole system would have collapsed. I have lost friends, and yesterday I lost my mom," his voice broke when he said it. "But here we are, gathered in this court massaging the ego of someone who I thought was my best friend," he started walking slowly around the room, looking everyone in their eye. It was hard to take my eyes off him.

"When did we become like this? When did we decide to stop helping each other and just look out for ourselves? The whole world, as we know it, has ended and yet nothing has changed, but that doesn't need to be our defining moment. We can change, starting right now!"

Nobody cheered; nobody even moved, they were all still focusing on the gunmen, even though their guns weren't drawn.

When Cole had started to speak, I had felt hope. I hung on every word he was saying and knew they were true; the problem wasn't what he was saying, the problem was that we were in a room full of greedy people who didn't like being told that they had been wrong. He was one man going against the ideologies of thousands of people who clung onto tiny slivers of nobility in their personal causes and ignored all the harm their actions caused. These people defended their wrongs with the argument that it wasn't their intention. It was the ultimate catch 22: if we left them to continue their selfish endeavours we would no longer be contributing to the problem, but by not doing something to resolve the problem we were ultimately part of it. So, I drew my line, because I wouldn't let my friend stand alone. I knew how to stop them. I knew how to make them listen; all it would take is a simple lie.

"He's trying to save you!" I screamed as all the attention turned to me.

"He told us the plan!" there were a few murmurs in the crowd as I pointed to Elon, "they've been watching all of you; drugging you, making you less aware as they steal all your belongings on the surface!"

The murmurs got louder.

The Cost of Good Intentions

"All the houses in Nod have been looted; we were there! We saw!"

A few people started to shout.

Elon was telling everyone to calm down, that none of it was true, but they weren't listening. They only cared about their possessions.

The guards had raised their weapons, but nobody cared. They kept on shouting and screaming, it was deafening.

Everyone was standing now, but they weren't cheering. Some people were trying to leave the court, I took it as an opportunity to get to Cole. I had just reached him when there was a gasp and a moment of silence as I heard a gun go off. I looked towards the door and saw a body lying on the floor in front of a soldier who had his gun aimed in the space where the person would have stood.

I grabbed Cole's arm as everyone shouted and screamed, they streamed towards the exit. He pulled me into him, and we held each other as people were pushing and shoving trying to get ahead of everyone else. It was pandemonium. I looked over Cole's shoulder to see Elon and Athena being surrounded as people tried to get through the shield of men that guarded their leader. They steadily moved towards the door, people following them, leaving the two of us, still clutching on to each other as we stood surrounded by hundreds of dead bodies.

I could hear the shouting and screaming continue in the distance, getting softer and softer as the crowd got further away. We walked, following them. Looking at all the destruction they left in their wake. Every single corridor was littered with bodies, some didn't have bullet holes, they were trampled during the human stampede. It was so clear to see where they had been.

Each room now had all of its contents broken. The same sights that had been beautiful to look at were now in pieces scattered across the floor. We looked into the Art Centre. The paintings were ruined, the books had their pages ripped out. The table was cracked, and the chairs broken. The beach area was no longer bright. There was a hole in the screen that had a display of the sun, when you looked through the hole you could see the metal beams that supported the screen. The Wall of Sacrifice was destroyed, the stone bench in pieces, and glass from the screen that displayed the field covered the floor. The cafeteria area had all the tables flipped upside down. The whiteboard laid in a corner of the room, a few of the lights were broken. The servant's quarters had all the doors ripped off their hinges. The smell was rife. The only room that remained untouched was the room with the cages. Nobody wanted to look at the result of their actions. Nobody wanted to even acknowledge that these people had their lives stolen from them. I heard a whimpering coming from the room.

"Amelia?" my father said.

I looked at Cole, unsure what to do. He could tell I was questioning myself.

"The only way to end all of this," he gestured to all the bodies around us, "and to really move forward, is to forgive and to drop the weapon."

"But look at what he's done, Cole," I whispered, fighting back tears, "he's just as much to blame."

The Cost of Good Intentions

"Look at what I've done, Amelia, and you gave me another chance. Nobody can change unless you give them the chance to."
"But what if he just carries on, the way he always has?"
"You need to believe that he won't, or else there isn't anything left to fight for. You have an opportunity to show him what's really important; you have an opportunity to make him see that there are good people left in this world."
I smiled at him; he handed me the keys to the cell before I walked into the room.
"Dad, I'm here."
"Amelia!" he was crying, "I heard so many people and gunshots and I was so worried about you."
"It's okay, I am okay," I started crying as well.
"I'm so sorry, sweetheart, I just wanted to make sure you would be safe. I kept worrying that Eleanor was going to do something to you if I didn't listen."
I could hear Cole breathe heavily behind me. I knew how hard it was for someone to speak like that about someone you cared about. He was silent as I opened the cage.
My dad got up and hugged me. He squeezed me so hard I felt I might break.
"We need to go," I managed to say.
He eased his grip before letting go of me all together. He only took notice of Cole when he did, he looked scared, like Cole might do something to him. I saw how wide his eyes were before Cole spoke.
"Let's get out of here,"
I watched as my dad visibly relaxed.

The Cost of Good Intentions

We walked to the elevator, the doors had been forced open, we stared at the elevator shaft before Cole pressed the button to recall the elevator from the surface.

When we got to the surface the carnage hadn't stopped. There weren't bodies here but the whole of Elon's back garden had been ruined. As we walked down the street, we saw that all the cars had been badly damaged, their bonnets had dents, their windows and mirrors were shattered, some of the tires had been slashed.

All the damage made a traceable path to the more expensive side of town, with the streets looking orderly the closer the three of us got to Cole's apartment.

When we got to his apartment, we returned to the gruesome scene of the bodies of the captain lying on the floor and Brad in the corner. Both of which had started to decay.

I watched as Cole took a seat on his bed, next to an empty bottle of vodka. He picked up the bottle, observing it closely before throwing it against the wall and watching it shatter into a million tiny pieces.

My dad just stood, looking around at the scene before him, while I walked to the kitchen and looked for food. We shared two cans of beans between us, and some sweets as we sat in silence.

CHAPTER 26

COLE

We sat in my apartment for a few hours. Ben spoke to Amelia, about all that he had done in the time that they had been apart. He took pride in talking about his part in designing various rooms in Elex and explaining his thought process, which genuinely seemed to have her at the centre of everything, when he came up with different ideas. I watched as they laughed and bonded, not caring about anything other than the fact that they were together. Nothing else mattered. I wondered if me and my mom could have ever had a moment like that. It hurt to think about. For all the wrong that she had done I knew how sorry she was for all of it when she laid there breathing her last breath, I could see it in her eyes. I watched as she realized that none of it mattered, that she had wasted her life trying to get all this power and really stand out amongst everyone else instead of taking the time to nurture our relationship. Over time the name Eleanor Clay will be forgotten in the minds of everyone else, but I would never forget her for the rest of my life. It was bittersweet to recollect all the time we had spent together growing up, as each memory was tainted by the selfishness of her actions.

She was just one of many selfish people though. I thought about Athena, a woman who had seen first hand what had happened on the surface because of Elex. She was so quick in taking up a role alongside Elon, the moment she could.

The Cost of Good Intentions

No matter her motivation it was clear to see that the underlying factor was power. She was given the opportunity and took it with both hands, not realizing that she was as much of a pawn as the rest of us. She would be a slave to the system that ruled Elex, because if she didn't agree to do what the system deemed necessary, she would have been another name on that terrible monument while someone else took her place, someone willing to do what she wouldn't.

I wasn't sure where we were going to go, or what we were going to do.

Everything was chaotic, there was no telling how far the effects of what had happened in Elex would spread. I wasn't even sure how the rest of the world, outside of Nod had been affected. There was no clear indication that anything would ever return to the way it was before, and maybe that was a good thing. I couldn't take the thought of going back to doing things that were unimportant, for people who didn't care about anything but themselves. In a strange way, I thought that, maybe this is what the world needed. A darkness that made the light shine upon all the things we choose to ignore.

I felt optimistic for the first time in a while. The future was uncertain, but I had my choice back, and I wanted to choose to do better, to be better.

I felt a warmth in my chest, before that warmth was put out by the bloody figure of Elon standing in my doorway as he pointed a gun at me.

Amelia and Ben had stopped talking, their eyes completely drawn to him.

The Cost of Good Intentions

He was covered in blood from top to bottom, but he didn't look like he was hurt.

His face contorted into an image of pure hatred.

"I gave you a chance. I paid for your pathetic life to be one filled with all the comfort you have lacked since I've known you, and this is how you repay me?"

I didn't feel any fear when I looked at him, I didn't care that he held the power to end my life in his hands, because I knew that I couldn't just sit back and take it anymore, I had to fight back.

"You let thousands of people get slaughtered to fulfil some sick fantasy of yours, and I didn't want any part in that."

"I told you, the pla-"

"Don't try to pretend that this is about anything other than power. I loved you like a brother, and yet you clearly didn't care about me. If you cared, you would have helped me break an addiction you knew I was struggling with, instead of encouraging it. You would have been honest about Beck from the start. You would have stopped lying to me when I gave you a second chance after you told me all about your involvement in Elex, and most of all, you wouldn't have tried to pay for my silence when you'd just murdered my mother!"

"I was trying to make things right!" Elon's hands were shaking.

"Bullshit! You were trying to cover up your crimes! No amount of comfort is worth that. Look around, all these bodies are your doing, all that blood on you is yours to keep."

"Don't act so high and mighty, Mole!" Elon spat the words out, thinking that they could hurt me after all that

I'd been through, "I know all about that homeless man you killed."

"See, that's the difference, yes, I killed that man. I didn't mean to, and I've regretted it ever since. I have tortured myself everyday thinking about the look on his face when it happened, and I'm still sorry. I still feel the guilt and the hurt because I know the pain I've caused. But I've tried everyday to make that right, while you have spent everyday continuing to hurt and destroy and not care about anyone other than yourself."

"Shut up!" Elon screamed, tears clearing some of the blood from his cheeks.

"No, I won-"

Elon pulled the trigger.

I felt the bullet hit my chest.

Amelia screamed and rushed to me. Ben sat on the floor in shock. Elon turned and ran away, just like his dad had.

I looked into Amelia's emerald green eyes. I could see the heartbreak in them.

"It's okay," I whispered.

My chest burned as I felt each breath was getting harder to take.

"Cole, I can't take it, it hurts too much. Please, don't leave me."

Her face was so red, and her eyes so full of tears, and I just wanted to take all of her pain away. I knew that I was the lucky one. I had broken my chains and slayed my own demons. My fight was coming to an end, but she would have to continue; she would have to finish what we had started together.

"This world will only break you if you let it. Carry on being kind. Carry on showing people that there is another way, like you showed me," I smiled at her, a tear formed in my left eye.
"Cole."
It was the last word that I heard. Her lips curving so delicately to form each letter as her tears fell from her face. She was my last thought before I closed my eyes for the very last time.

EPILOGUE

AMELIA

I wore a sundress with sunflowers scattered all over. We drove in a shitty Kia Picanto in the early hours of a Sunday morning. Stand By Me by Ben E. King blasted through the speakers. I looked beside me at my dad, dressed in a suit. There were three sets of flowers on the back seat, an assortment of all the brightest flowers we could find. We drove the same way that we had in all the previous Sundays for the past 11 months.

The world had moved on since the day we lost Cole Clay. It didn't even take long for it to happen. There was no trace of Elon or Athena anywhere, even after I had pointed some new police officers in the direction of the cave. They had said it was empty, no sign of anything or anyone.

The rest of the world had been unaffected by all that had happened in Nod. I found it hard to believe that nobody knew anything about what was going on for months, I'm sure they were covering it up. Maybe Nod was just a trial. We got a new president, the old one had been murdered the day that the sun went missing, just before the emergency broadcasts were aired on every television in Nod.

The new president got help from neighbouring countries, they sent all different kinds of people to help restore power to the grid and help us get back to day-to-day life. He then declared the day that the sun went missing as a national holiday, where we would spend the day remembering all those affected by the terrible tragedy that saw millions of people lose their lives. We were instructed to all wear black on that day.

Nod was on the news every day, with headlines on the screen making it all look like some big accident. Largely pinning all the things that they couldn't cover up on Elon.

We drove through the iron gates of the cemetery.

I looked out of the window at the outlines of all the gravestones as we continued along the short path to the parking.

My dad parked the car, we were the only ones there, and we got out. I grabbed the flowers from the back seat and walked to my dad who was waiting at the pedestrian's entrance.

He held out his hand. I took it, after I had given him a set of flowers.

"She would be proud of you," he said as we began to walk.

It took me a minute to realize he had meant my mother, and not Eleanor.

"I used to listen to her speak to you when she was pregnant with you, she used to wait until she thought I was asleep and then she would whisper, 'you're going to be the best one, the best one they've ever seen. My sweet girl, I can feel the warmth of your love already'," he smiled as he recalled the memory.

We walked until we reached the spot. In the middle of all of them, no real distinction between their stones and the others. It was the biggest crime that Cole Clay and Rory Egan were buried amongst the masses when they deserved so much more.

The Cost of Good Intentions

My eyes drifted from left to right as I observed each headstone in turn.

I had been in charge of coming up with the epitaphs.

Rory's read, "in loving memory of a lost spirit who has finally found his way home."

Cole's read, "In loving memory of a wonderful son, friend and hero. A bright light in the darkest of nights."

I placed a set of flowers in front of each of their graves, and watched as my dad placed a set on top of Eleanor's grave, which was right next to Cole's.

We stood in silence, our hands clasped in front of us with our heads lowered as we paid our respects.

"Could I have a moment alone, before we go, please dad?"

"Of course," his eyes softened as he looked at me. "Take all the time you need."

I watched as he walked away, bowing his head as he did. When he was out of sight I sighed as I sat down in front of Cole's headstone.

"Everything's just gone back to normal since you've been gone, and it's so hard without you here. I feel so alone, every day, and there's nothing I can do to stop it. It doesn't matter that they gave us all we would ever need for the rest of our lives. I just miss you so much, and I would trade it all for another day with you," I started crying, "I wish you met Rory. I wish that we could have all spent time laughing and joking with each other as we grew old. I dream of it sometimes, but then I wake up and there's a huge hole in me, and I don't know how to fill it. It gets worse when I realize that nobody will ever really know all the sacrifices you made for them, and I get so angry because they didn't deserve it, any of it. I sit and replay the memories in my head and think about all the things we could have done differently, but none of it brings you back. Any of you," I looked at all the tombstones, "I don't know what else to do but sit here and talk to you and think about the past," I wiped the tears from my eyes as I stood up.

I walked back towards the car. My dad was sitting inside. He started the car when I got in, the engine sputtered as it came to life.

We drove out of the cemetery and headed back towards our house.

"I heard what you said, back there, to your friend," he said as he drove.

I looked at him, not saying anything.

"It's okay to feel alone, you know?" he continued, "but you need to know that you've got me. There are other good people around, they are just hard to find, but you need to know that they're there. I want you to know that it's okay to think about the past, I do it every day, and I regret a lot. But from what you've told me of your friend, I think we came to the same conclusion."

"And what's that?" I asked.

"That at some point you have to make sure that you don't look back on what you're doing now in the same way."

We sat in silence when I saw it. It was just over the peak of the hill we were driving towards.

I felt warmth as I squinted my eyes and soaked in the first rays of sunlight of a new day.

ACKNOWLEDGEMENTS

Here we are, at the end of the first of many. I cannot believe that I have reached this point after what feels like a lifetime. The process has been a long and testing experience but one that has brought me an immeasurable sense of pleasure. So, without further ado I would like to start my thanks by thanking the most important influence in all of our lives, being God, without whom none of us would be able to do anything. To my partner in crime and ultimate supporter throughout this process, Karolina, who put up with my hermit like behaviour and encouraged me with an endless stream of delicious food and moral support. To my Dad, who has provided me with my most valuable asset to date, perspective. To my Mom, who had no idea about anything but has always wholeheartedly encouraged me to pursue my dreams. To my Sister who, without knowing it, reignited my spark by sending me pieces of cringe worthy writing that I had created many years ago. The aforementioned have each had direct influence during the writing process of this novel, but throughout my life I have been influenced by so many people who I hold close to my heart. I constantly recollect memories of times passed and some of them bring about periods of poignant reflection, some are humbling, some are breathtaking, some are inspiring and continue to motivate me to this day. I will never have enough pages to express my deepest thanks to all the people in those memories but if you read this and recollect a moment we shared, whether it is a painful memory or one that you happily recall from time to time, you have been instrumental to the creation of this novel. To you, the reader, I would like to thank you for taking the time to read my story, I can only hope that you have enjoyed it and that you look forward to my future creations.

Printed in Great Britain
by Amazon